The Executioner expected to die a violent death someday

But the civilians in the lobby had not signed up for battle pay, and if Bolan failed in the action he had to take within the next few seconds, they would surely die.

The bomber had almost reached the CIA man when the Executioner turned around.

As Bolan increased his pace to catch up with the man in the vest, the CIA agent moved smoothly into the bomber's path and grabbed both of his wrists. Bolan drew his fixed-blade knife from behind his back and raised it high over his head. All other movement in the lobby had stopped.

The bomber screamed something in Arabic as Bolan dived through the air, the blade clenched in a reverse grip. As he collided with the man's back, he brought the blade down with all his strength, penetrating the man's skull.

A few gasps came from around the lobby. Then the screams of men and women filled the air. Bolan pried the blade out of the bomber's skull and wiped it on the back of the man's vest before turning him over.

"Murderers!" a high-pitched female voice shouted. "Call the police."

The Executioner unzipped the bomber's vest and a collective gasp came from the crowd when the people saw a good two-dozen sticks of dynamite strapped to the dead man's body.

There were no more accusations of homicide.

MACK BOLAN ®
The Executioner

The Executioner

Don Pendleton's ®

FINAL COUP

A GOLD EAGLE BOOK FROM

WORLDWIDE ®

TORONTO • NEW YORK • LONDON
AMSTERDAM • PARIS • SYDNEY • HAMBURG
STOCKHOLM • ATHENS • TOKYO • MILAN
MADRID • WARSAW • BUDAPEST • AUCKLAND

Recycling programs
for this product may
not exist in your area.

First edition March 2011

ISBN-13: 978-0-373-64388-2

Special thanks and acknowledgment to
Jerry VanCook for his contribution to this work.

FINAL COUP

Copyright © 2011 by Worldwide Library.

Printed in U.S.A.

Democracy is worth dying for, because it's the most deeply honorable form of government ever devised by man.

—Ronald Reagan
1911–2004

All people have a right to live and die freely. Anyone who dares to take that away will face my wrath and suffer inevitable defeat. That's a promise.

—Mack Bolan

THE
MACK BOLAN
LEGEND

Nothing less than a war could have fashioned the destiny of the man called Mack Bolan. Bolan earned the Executioner title in the jungle hell of Vietnam.

But this soldier also wore another name—Sergeant Mercy. He was so tagged because of the compassion he showed to wounded comrades-in-arms and Vietnamese civilians.

Mack Bolan's second tour of duty ended prematurely when he was given emergency leave to return home and bury his family, victims of the Mob. Then he declared a one-man war against the Mafia.

He confronted the Families head-on from coast to coast, and soon a hope of victory began to appear. But Bolan had broken society's every rule. That same society started gunning for this elusive warrior—to no avail.

So Bolan was offered amnesty to work within the system against terrorism. This time, as an employee of Uncle Sam, Bolan became Colonel John Phoenix. With a command center at Stony Man Farm in Virginia, he and his new allies—Able Team and Phoenix Force—waged relentless war on a new adversary: the KGB.

But when his one true love, April Rose, died at the hands of the Soviet terror machine, Bolan severed all ties with Establishment authority.

Now, after a lengthy lone-wolf struggle and much soul-searching, the Executioner has agreed to enter an "arm's-length" alliance with his government once more, reserving the right to pursue personal missions in his Everlasting War.

It was hardly the way Mack Bolan had expected the mission to begin.

When the sudden explosion of rifle-fire blew past him on both sides, the man known as the Executioner drew the .44 Magnum Desert Eagle from the Kydex hip holster beneath his navy blue blazer. He automatically crouched into a classic "point shooting" position as his eyes scanned the Yaounde, Cameroon, airport terminal with the speed of lightning, looking for a target to return fire.

At the same time, he wondered what had gone wrong.

As it always did in times of grave danger, the Executioner's mind geared into overdrive, working at the speed of light, and outdistancing even the most sophisticated computers. His brain took in the information provided by his senses, processed it all in a thousandth of a second and began kicking out potential answers to the assault.

Bolan saw a small movement in a second-story window of the terminal, and at the same time a flash of light. The sun had just bounced off what had to be the lens of a rifle scope.

The target was beyond the distance for point shooting, so Bolan rose into a classic isosceles stance and lined up the

Desert Eagle's sights. He squeezed the trigger, sending his first .44 Magnum jacketed lead round toward the flash of light, while his mind continued to process the information it was receiving.

Who were the shooters? The sniper rifle scope and the rapid autofire didn't go together. That told him there was at least one more man shooting at them.

But why had the onslaught begun in the first place? Bolan didn't know. But one thing was certain: they knew what they were doing.

They had waited until all of the men who'd accompanied him had walked down the steps of the jet before opening fire. That, in turn, told the Executioner two more things.

Word of their coming had preceded their arrival.

And the enemy knew exactly how many men were on board.

Somewhere there was a deadly leak in security. But finding it would have to take a backseat to what was happening at the moment. Before he even thought about the mole, the Executioner and the other men had to survive this surprise attack.

Another rifle barrel poked out of a second-floor window of the terminal, roughly a hundred yards away. With both hands gripping the Desert Eagle, Bolan took careful aim once more and gently squeezed the trigger. As all distant and precisely aimed shots should, his second Magnum round came as a slight surprise. He had aimed at the top of the window, but the bullet drop at that distance sent the lethal, fragmenting hollowpoint round into a blurry headlike shape just above the rifle. Almost exactly like the first sniper had done a second earlier, whoever held this weapon fell backward, out of sight. But not before he had dropped his long gun from the window, and sent a shot of residual blood and brain tissue after it.

One down. But how many to go? The soldier had no way of knowing.

Bolan looked quickly around him. Most of the men who had accompanied him were from the U.S. Secret Service, and their hands had found Glocks, SIG-Sauers or Berettas. Dr. John Lareby—an expert in counterterrorism, guerrilla warfare, survival and executive protection—and the only representative of the CIA within the group—held a modest little Walther PPK .380 in his fist.

More shots rang out, and one of them ripped the shoulder out of Bolan's jacket. Beneath its path, the soldier felt the heat and a slight sting. It had been ability and training, but also a good deal of luck, that he had spotted either of the two shooters. Although he could hear more gunfire and feel other bullets whizzing past to make loud clinks in the body of the plane, it was impossible to determine the exact points of origin.

Bolan knew they had only two choices: they could sprint toward the terminal and try to get below the line of fire, or they could retreat into, or behind, the plane.

It didn't take long for him to determine which option made more sense. There was still a football field between them and the terminal, and the chances of him, Lareby and the Secret Service agents all running into the fire without getting killed was slim to say the least.

"Get back!" Bolan yelled, and a moment later he and the rest of the Americans had hit the ground and were rolling beneath the plane. By the time they were on the other side, a few shots continued coming at them, hitting the tarmac next to the Concorde and ricocheting past their feet.

The Executioner moved toward the rear of the aircraft. Peering around one of the tail fins he stared toward the terminal. A pause had come in the shooting, and Bolan suspected the gunmen were planning their next strategy. As

Lareby and the Secret Service agents crowded around him, the Executioner waited, thinking, taking in received data and combining it with what was happening, his thoughts racing through his brain at the speed of light.

But then the gunfire, which had disappeared for a few minutes, suddenly returned with a vengeance. Bolan, Lareby and the Secret Service agents who had again crowded around him, ducked back away from the tail of the plane and waited. A few random shots skidded beneath the jet, but the majority of fire just punched more holes in the fuselage.

Bolan's mind flashed to the man who had piloted them to Cameroon. Jack Grimaldi was an old friend, fellow warrior and arguably the best pilot in the world. He was the only man who had not exited the plane, and he would have taken refuge behind the cockpit, where shields of bullet-resistant Kevlar and steel plating had been installed along the walls. The Executioner grinned slightly as he pictured the man in his mind's eye. At this moment, Grimaldi would have his beloved Smith & Wesson Model 66 out of its holster and gripped in his right hand. In his left would be a pair of .38/357 speedloaders.

Both would be loaded with RBCD total fragmentation .357 rounds.

Should everything else go south, and Bolan, Lareby and the Secret Service agents were killed, Grimaldi would take out as many of the assailants as he could before the jet was rushed and he, too, was shot. Like the captain of a seagoing vessel, Grimaldi would go down with his "ship."

Grimaldi's primary contribution to America and the rest of the free world were his aviation skills. He could fly everything from a kite to a space shuttle. But he was as much a warrior at heart as any of the other men accompanying Bolan.

And he'd die like one if he had to.

As the gunfire continued, the Executioner decided to wait them out. Sometimes doing nothing was doing something, and the best course of action. Sooner or later, the shooters were going to run out of ammo. Or perhaps the local police or the military would arrive to send them scattering back to whatever rocks they'd crawled out from under.

For the time being, however, the best plan of action was no plan of action. And *that* was the hardest thing a true soldier ever had to do.

The Executioner's mind raced back once more over what had happened during the past few days. The Cameroonian president, Robert Menye, was on the run, having abandoned his position of leadership the same day the International Criminal Court—ICC—issued arrest warrants for his war crimes. An emergency election had been called for under the Cameroon constitution, and the suddenly growing Cameroon People's Union had continued to combine with a whole new lot of men awakening to nationalism amid the turbulence. In short the Cameroon People's Union and the Kamerun National Democratic Party had both named candidates.

Cameroon's prime minister—the only man left with any power during the chaos—had frantically called upon the U.S. President for help. The man in the White House had sent Secret Service agents to spearhead the protection of both candidates. The CIA, for its part, had sent Lareby, who was being billed as a so-called observer.

And Bolan. Who wasn't on the grid as anything except a Department of Justice agent named Matt Cooper. Not even the Secret Service agents or CIA field operative John Lareby knew any more about him.

Except that he was in charge. And that his orders were not to be questioned.

The pungent odor of jet fuel began to fill the Executioner's nostrils, and suddenly the new tack the shooters were taking became clear to him. They had shot hundreds of rounds that had dented but bounced off the reinforced sides of the plane. But somewhere along the way the fuel storage walls—despite being reinforced with Kevlar and steel—had been penetrated.

The Executioner was reminded that the proper adjective for items such as Kevlar and steel plates was "bullet-resistant" not "bulletproof." One or more of the snipers either had a tremendously powerful rifle, or a multitude of lesser calibers had all hit in the same area, eventually wearing down the protective shielding.

As he stared at the ground beneath the wing, the Executioner heard more rounds explode. A small flame started beneath the plane. At almost the same time, Lareby shouted out, "We've got to get out of here! This thing's going up in about half a minute!"

Bolan ignored the warning. But in his peripheral vision he saw several of the Secret Service agents sprinting away from the plane, farther from the snipers in the terminal. Hurrying toward the cabin, the soldier pulled himself up and in through the opened window.

Grimaldi was not in the pilot's seat, but Bolan hadn't expected him to be. As he started to enter the still-open doorway into the plane, a pair of strong arms reached up and grabbed him, surprising the Executioner, and tugged him back to the ground.

The soldier turned toward the man who had just pulled him back and saw it was a young blond-haired Secret Service agent. He couldn't remember the man's name.

"Forget the pilot!" the young man screamed. "He's toast!"

Before he even realized what he was doing, Bolan slammed a right cross into the Secret Service man's chin, which sent him into dreamland on the tarmac. Then he looked at the nearer of the other Secret Service agents. "I may have to carry the pilot out of here," he shouted above the continuing roar of rifle-fire. "Which means that if I have to knock you out, too, there won't be anyone left to carry the two of you. Do you get my drift?"

"We get it," one of the agents said, then stooped to begin trying to lift the unconscious man into his arms.

"Good," Bolan said. He holstered the Desert Eagle, turned back toward the plane and climbed aboard once more.

Grimaldi was exactly where Bolan knew he'd be. His back rested against the side of the fuselage. Blood was splattered all over the cabin, and dark red stains dripped down behind the pilot. "Whoever said this was bullet-resistant," the pilot said in dry humor, "might have been stretching the truth a little."

Bolan hurried toward him. "How bad are you hit, Jack?" he asked.

"Not all that bad, I don't think. One round in the chest. High above the heart. The other one's in my leg. Dangerously close to the femoral artery. But like they say, a miss is as good as a mile." He coughed. "It tore through my pants, barely missing a part of my anatomy that I'd just as soon die as lose."

"Then let's get you out of here so you can use it again," Bolan responded.

Grimaldi shook his head. "Uh-uh, Sarge. I can smell the gas and I know there's fire. This thing's going to blow any second. You'll never make it carrying me. Take off. On your own. There's no point in both of us dying."

"Neither one of us is going to die," Bolan said as he reached down, grabbed Grimaldi's hand, pulled him up and threw him over his shoulder in a classic fireman's carry.

"Well, if we both get vaporized in the next two seconds, don't blame me," the pilot said.

But Bolan wasn't listening. He made his way to the doorway, opened it and looked down, surprised to see the Secret Service agents waiting. The man with the blond brush cut was awake again. He had a swollen chin, which had turned red and promised to be black and blue by tomorrow. But he didn't seem angry.

The soldier dropped down to the tarmac and yelled over the continuing gunfire, "Go! Get out of here. Do it!"

The men turned and took off away from the plane. The Executioner—with Grimaldi still over his shoulder—followed. He was well aware of the fact that the farther they got behind the plane, the better targets they provided for the snipers. But taking the chance of being hit by a bullet at that range was far smarter than awaiting certain death when the fire finally reached the aircraft's fuel tanks.

They were roughly 150 yards from the aircraft when it finally exploded.

Bolan set Grimaldi on the tarmac and turned back toward the plane. Flames and smoke rose high enough to hide them no matter how skilled, how well-armed the snipers were—or how many of them were out there.

"So much for our low-profile entry into the country," Lareby said. Bolan watched him as he stared back at the flames jumping from what was quickly beginning to look like a fiery dinosaur skeleton in a museum. The fire had spread to all parts of the plane.

Lareby knelt next to where Grimaldi sat. "Better check you out, sport," he said. "Hold still. I'm a physician, after all."

"Then get to work and prove it," Grimaldi came back. "But I'm okay, seriously."

"You're okay for the moment," Lareby said. "But in about ten minutes the adrenaline is going to wear off, and you'll feel like someone jammed a hot branding iron through you."

"I've lived through worse than this before," the pilot said.

Bolan had been too busy to notice Lareby's black leather bag. But he watched as the man pulled out a stethoscope, a hypodermic needle and a small vial. "What are you giving him?" he asked in a stern voice.

"Morphine," Lareby said. "He's right—his wounds aren't life-threatening. The material in the ballistic siding slowed the bullets, and you couldn't have asked for cleaner shots. Upper chest, then on out the back. Missed the lung. Worse-case scenario, it may have chipped a shoulder blade."

"How about the leg wound?" Bolan pressed.

"He won't be running any marathons for a while," the CIA man said. "But it's nothing. The blood's already starting to coagulate."

"I said I was all right," Grimaldi said as the tried to get up off the ground. This time Bolan helped Lareby hold him back down, twisting him onto his back.

Only then did Bolan see how much pain there actually was in his old friend's eyes. But the eyes were the only place it showed. His face looked more angry than hurt.

"They had to be loaded up with armor-piercing rounds," Lareby said as he probed further at the pilot below him. "The wound channel is so straight you could stick a pencil through it. Hardly any tissue damage to the sides of the bullet's path." The CIA doctor pulled off the cap on the hypodermic needle with his teeth, spit it to the side, then punctured the top of the tiny vial with the needle. Holding it upward, he injected Grimaldi's arm with the morphine and, one by one, Bolan watched the wrinkles in the Stony Man pilot's face smooth out as the drug hit his system.

Grimaldi finally grinned. "You know," he said. "On second thought, I think the adrenaline *is* wearing off. You wouldn't by any chance have a six-pack of that stuff you can leave with me?" His tongue suddenly loosened, Grimaldi continued with, "They got any flowers around here?" he asked jokingly. "I'm getting this uncontrollable urge to wear flowers in my hair and go to San Francisco."

Bolan and Lareby hauled Grimaldi to his feet. "Sorry, Flower Child," Bolan said. "But Timothy Leary's dead and the Age of Aquarius is long gone."

"Maybe for *you,* Sarge." Grimaldi laughed. He was standing on his own now, but his feet were still wobbly. "But I've got all of Janice Joplin, Blind Faith and Cream on CDs back in my car. It's to drown out the 'rap' I have to endure at stoplights." He frowned for a moment, scratching his chin. "Or they might be in my room back at the main house. But I'm gonna look until I find them and—"

Bolan cleared his throat. "Jack?" he said.

"Yeah?" the pilot said.

"No more morphine-speak, okay? Just shut up."

Grimaldi lost his grin. "Gotcha," he said.

A moment later, Bolan had taken him by the arm and was moving him backward, farther away from the fiery plane. When he had gotten the pilot out of earshot of the other men, Bolan turned to look at them.

They all stared back. And unless he missed his guess, they were all wondering just what the "main house" was.

Jack Grimaldi had realized his mistake even before Bolan spoke, and he said, "Sorry, Sarge. I guess I could blame it on the morphine, but that's no excuse."

Bolan turned his back to the rest of the men in case any of them read lips. "It's no big deal, Jack," he said. "But these guys are paid to be suspicious of anybody and everybody. Look at it from their point of view for a moment. We suddenly appear, seemingly out of nowhere, and they get orders directly from the White House that we're in charge. And while we know all about them, they know *nothing* about us. We've got to be cautious."

Grimaldi nodded. "Rest assured it won't happen again, big guy," he said. "I suppose I'll have to get checked out by some hospital here. But from now on my only topic of conversation around strangers will be my health."

The Executioner smiled. "One slipup in…how many years have we been working together?"

"More than I'd like to count," Grimaldi said.

Bolan chuckled under his breath. "It's time to regroup and replan." He took Grimaldi by the arm and guided him back toward the rest of the Americans.

By now, the flames and smoke from the jet were dying down, and they'd soon be visible targets again. With absolutely no cover or concealment on the vast, wide-open runway. The sounds of gunfire from the terminal had all but vanished, but Bolan didn't kid himself.

The snipers had not fled the area. They, like Bolan himself, were waiting for the smoke to clear before they resumed fire. And as he half-carried Grimaldi farther from the inferno, the fog began to disperse.

And the soldier saw a half-dozen Cameroonian army jeeps racing toward them.

That was the greeting he'd been briefed to expect, but he'd had no advance intel that it would be during a pitched gun battle.

For a brief moment, the Executioner glanced back at the skeletal aircraft. The fire and smoke was close to burning itself out, which meant that he had to get all his men away from what was about to become a disaster zone.

The smoke continued to float apart in the air as they advanced, allowing Bolan a better view of where they were headed. But it was a mixed blessing. The clearing air also allowed the snipers to pick out their targets again, and the blasts from the rifles in the windows of the terminal building came back with a vengeance.

The fog had all but been left behind them when Bolan spotted the corrugated steel shack between the runways. It stood at an angle that would be difficult to shoot at from the terminal and, with the wounded men, it appeared to be their best objective. It would not stop high-powered rifle rounds but if they could get behind its walls, it would at least keep the enemy from locking in on specific targets.

Specific targets meaning human beings.

Them.

Bolan began to run toward the small building as the bullets from the snipers' scoped rifles spit past him. With Grimaldi still in tow, he utilized a "serpentine" tactic, running an S pattern that changed in speed, shape and size so that it became no true pattern at all. Behind him, he could hear the other men following.

The soldier dropped Grimaldi to the grass as soon as he was behind the shack. And then, just as suddenly as it had started, the rifle-fire ceased. Bolan glanced around the corner of the building and saw why.

On both sides, as well as behind the terminal, stood a ten-foot-high chain-link fence. Topped with coil after coil of rolled razor-wire, it was meant to stop or slow anyone trying to transverse it. It would be easy to scale the fence. But passing through the razor-wire without getting shredded to pieces—or at least tangled and providing an easy, stationary target for the sharpshooters in the terminal—would be all but impossible.

But the fence and wire didn't do a very good job of retarding the tank that was pushing slowly through it to the left of the runway where the jet's remains still stood. The armored vehicle began snapping the fence and the steel poles between, which it stretched as if they were dry wooden matchsticks.

Bolan stared at the tank for a moment. An older-model Chieftain, it was of British design and had obviously been left behind when Great Britain moved out of Cameroon. Originally meant for use by a legitimate new government, it had, not surprisingly, fallen into the hands of terrorists instead. Bolan knew that the Chieftain had been created as a result of Britain's World War II warfare experience. It was built to give priority to both firepower and armored protection.

The soldier felt the muscles in his face tighten. Earlier, he had had a brief moment of regret that his team's rifles, grenades, extra ammo, clothes and other gear had been left on the jet and were now either in ashes or otherwise useless. But watching the tank roll forward undeterred, he realized they had carried nothing that would stop the British Chieftain.

No, Bolan thought, as the jeeps arrived and their occupants began scooting closer to make room for the Americans. Until more firepower could arrive via diplomatic pouches, he and the other men would have only the weapons they had carried on them and anything they could beg, borrow, or steal from the Cameroonians.

Taking a seat next to the dark-skinned sergeant in one of the jeeps, Bolan held on to the top of his door as the man cut a sharp U-turn and picked up speed again. A 60 mm machine gun was mounted in each jeep, but they would be of little more use against the Chieftain than his .44 Magnum Desert Eagle. They led the convoy of jeeps to escape the inevitable aim of the tank's antitank rounds or machine gun—either of which could turn the jeeps into fiery infernos like the jet.

Bolan had learned many truths during his career as a warrior. And one of them was that when you were outgunned and unable to go toe-to-toe with a superior weapon itself, the only plan of action that had any chance of succeeding was to take out the man whose finger was on the trigger.

The soldier's eyebrows furrowed in concentration as a

head suddenly rose through the hatch on top of the tank. All Bolan could see was the man's hair and eyes.

The men inside would not be expecting any significant return fire from the Americans' pistols or the AK-47s carried by the Cameroonian regulars in the jeeps. So as soon as their speed had leveled off, Bolan twisted and rested the Desert Eagle on the side of the jeep. Aiming high, he lined up the front and rear sights of the big .44 Magnum pistol just above the head sticking out of the tank's hatch.

But before he could squeeze the trigger, he heard the boom of the Chieftain's gun and saw the tank literally thrown backward with the recoil.

What was left of the airplane finally crumbled into an unrecognizable mass of broken steel. Bolan tried to line up the Desert Eagle's sights again. But before he could shoot at the eyes and scalp he'd seen, the terrorist in the tank had disappeared into the vehicle.

Who *were* these assailants? Bolan couldn't help but wonder again. Were they Cameroonian People's Union or Kamerun Democratic National Party? He didn't know, but their attack was just as deadly no matter which side of the genocide they were on.

As the jeeps raced on, the rushing wind made conversation difficult. "We still having the meeting with the prime minister here at the airport?" Bolan shouted.

"The meeting is still scheduled," the sergeant behind the wheel yelled back to him. "But I doubt it will be here." He pointed toward the terminal and Bolan could see that it was rivaling the jet in the burning category.

Whoever was behind this "Welcome to Cameroon" fiasco was taking out the airport building as well as his plane.

"Who were we fighting?" Bolan finally got a chance to ask.

The sergeant shrugged as he answered. "Either the CPU

or the KDNP," he said. "Take your pick. They wear the same old combination of battle-dress uniforms and civilian clothes, and it's hard to tell who they are unless you can get them to talk. CPUs usually speak English with a heavy accent. KDNP-ers have the same accent but almost always speak French. Most, however, are bilingual."

By then the jeeps had slowed as they neared another set of buildings far from the terminal. Bolan guessed this to be the cargo plane landing area, and probably the airstrips used by the Cameroonian military forces. The structure was not nearly as architecturally pleasing or as well kept as the passengers' terminal had been, but it was in a lot better shape than that building was going to be for a long time after the flames died down.

The Executioner looked over his shoulder at the still-burning airplane, far in the distance now. The old adage "between the devil and the deep blue sea" crossed his mind. But, somehow, that old saying didn't quite sum up his, or his team's, current situation.

It seemed far more likely that they were between two different kinds of hell.

The Chieftain was even farther away now than it had been before it finished off the airplane. But it was still following the jeeps across the runways toward the rough commercial buildings. And the same hair and eyes had risen again through the hatch.

Finally on flatter land, the Executioner once again rested the Desert Eagle on the jeep's rear ledge and lined up the sights, allowing for even more bullet drop this time. Slowly, without allowing the big .44's barrel to waver in the slightest, he squeezed the trigger.

The "scream of the Eagle" was still in his ears as the head sticking out of the British tank literally exploded like a watermelon. The tank ground to a halt. Three more men inside the old and battered war vehicle panicked and, rather than remain within the relative safety of the tank, pushed the headless man out through the exit hole. Clad in a variety of different patterned camouflage, OD-green BDU pants and blouses, and T-shirts, jeans and khaki work pants, they followed the corpse and dropped to the ground.

Bolan picked off all three of them as their boots hit the tarmac. The advance of the tank had ended, and with that failure, the sporadic sniper shots, which had already begun to die down from the flaming terminal, ended too.

"Stop the jeep," Bolan ordered.

The driver hit the brakes.

The big American leaped from the jeep. The Desert Eagle still in his hand, he whirled in a quick 360-degree scan of the area.

The snipers he hadn't already killed had fled the fiery inferno that had once been the terminal building. And the four men who had managed the Chieftain were dead. But as the rest of his American team and the army troops hopped over the sides of their vehicles, Bolan knew one thing for certain.

The enemy might have drawn the short stick here, in this battle, but the war was far from over.

Bolan and his team jumped back into the jeep, and the driver led the convoy on.

2

The initial meeting with Prime Minister Jean Antangana, other chiefs of state, and Cameroonian cabinet members who had not fled with ex-President Robert Menye, had been transferred to the commercial area of the airport as soon as the gunfire had broken out. The jeeps stopped in front of a cruder, more industrial-looking Quonset hut.

Bolan had replenished the Desert Eagle with a full magazine and now held it in his right hand, resting across his lap. He took notice of the fact that John Lareby, who was seated in front of him in the jeep, still had his Walther unholstered, while he gripped Grimaldi's shoulder with his other hand.

The ace pilot had fallen asleep.

A swarthy man wearing the trappings of a colonel strutted out the front door and instinctively walked toward Bolan. "I am Colonel Luc Pierre Essam," he said as he shrugged back his shoulders in pride and extended his hand to the Executioner. "I am in charge of the military protection squads, and it was my men who just saved you."

Bolan just stared him in the eye as he transferred the Desert Eagle to his left hand and gripped Essam's.

It was CIA field agent Lareby who spoke next. "Well, I guess we can't thank you enough for clarifying that misconception, Colonel Essam," he said. "Until this minute, I'd have sworn that we pretty much saved ourselves."

The colonel's smile faded. There was an awkward pause, and then he stepped back and said, "If you please, gentlemen. We are set up in a private room inside the hut." He waved his hand toward the door.

Bolan hooked a thumb over his shoulder toward Grimaldi. "Our pilot needs medical attention," he said.

Colonel Essam nodded. "I have already called for ambulances," he said. "Your man will leave for the hospital in the first to arrive."

Bolan nodded his understanding, and he and the other men stepped down from the jeeps before following Essam into the building. Once inside, the Executioner finally holstered his .44. There was a short row of bunk beds that had been slept in but not made, and he had to remind himself that while tidiness was insisted upon to instill discipline in the armed forces of the U.S., that was not the case in many Third World countries.

Essam opened the door to a large room. Bolan led the way inside and saw a variety of men already seated around a long conference table. Some wore suits and ties. Others were decked out in dress uniforms or battle gear. But no two sets of BDUs matched—in some cases, not even the blouse and pants on the same soldiers.

In short, they were barely better dressed than the terrorists who had attacked the aircraft.

With oil, timber and coffee exports, Cameroon's economy was better than many other African nations. But "good" was a relative term. The mismatched uniforms meant the army was scrounging out its existence as best it could. And as mismatched as the uniforms were, Bolan knew from experience that with egomaniacs like Menye, the troops "ate first." He had yet to meet any of Cameroon's civilians, but he knew they would be in even worse shape than these military men.

The pompous Colonel Essam escorted Bolan to an empty chair just to the right of the head of the table. The other men found open seats among the Cameroonians still loyal to their prime minister.

"Gentlemen," Essam said as he moved to the head of the table but remained standing. "We are in what English-speaking people call 'dire straits.' Does everyone know what I mean by that?"

The men around the table nodded.

"Then I will turn this meeting over to Prime Minister Jean Antangana," Essam said. "But I would like to say one more thing first. To the men in this room who serve directly under me within the security force—the Americans who have just entered the room are in charge. And you will obey their orders. I do not like this any more than any other man would like having to call upon an outside nation for help, but that is, unfortunately, the case." He stopped speaking for a moment and looked toward Bolan. "I am sure the Americans understand our hesitancy."

Bolan, and the other newcomers to the room, nodded.

"Nevertheless," Essam restated, "that is the reality of the situation. We need their expertise, and they have graciously agreed to provide it." He stepped back from the seat and a coffee-colored man of mixed race, wearing a blue business suit, white shirt and paisley tie took his place.

Essam moved to the chair the man had just vacated, directly across from Bolan.

The soldier could see that the prime minister was sick before he even opened his mouth.

Jean Antangana cleared his throat and his chest sounded as if marbles were rattling around against one another. "For those of you who have graciously come to our aid, I thank you." Now that the man was standing, Bolan could see that Antangana's suit was at least two sizes too large. The bony features of his face, along with a slightly yellow tint to his tanned skin, furthered his observation that the man was seriously ill. And had been for a long time.

"We are facing hard times," Antangana finally went on. "Our president has left office and is on the run. Which, considering some of the outrageous actions he has taken, is not such a bad thing."

There were chuckles around the room, but they had a fearful ring to them.

"And we have two men running for office who may be even more evil than Menye was." He cleared his throat once more with the same peculiar rattling sound. When the spasm had passed, he said, "We cannot have this. Neither candidate, or party, is acceptable."

A man toward the end of the table wearing BDU pants and a soiled brown T-shirt butted in. "If I might be so bold," he said. "I see no reason not to kill them both."

Antangana shook his head. "That would do no good," he said. "Both the Cameroon People's Union and the Kamerun National Democratic Party would simply install other men in their place. Keep in mind that this is an *emergency* election, and candidates are allowed to file right up to the day before the election."

"Sir," a black man wearing a lightweight tropical suit said, "why don't *you* file for the position?" He cleared his throat nervously. "I am sure all of the men in this room would support you."

There was a murmur of assent around the room.

"I cannot do that," Antangana said in his gravelly voice. "You all know why."

Bolan didn't know exactly why, and he knew the other

Americans who had flown with him from Washington, D.C., to Cameroon didn't either. But he could guess.

The Executioner was no medical doctor like Lareby. But it didn't take an "M.D." after your name to see that some form of cancer was eating Antangana down to the bone. Bolan guessed that the man viewed the unification of Cameroon under a true democracy with a fair and honest president as the last great deed he could perform for his homeland before he died.

Antangana seemed to read the soldier's mind. Turning toward Bolan, he made the man's suspicions a reality. "I am sorry," the prime minister said. "For saying that *everyone* in this room knows why I cannot run for office. To our new friends from America, I have throat cancer. It has spread, and continues to do so at an alarming rate."

Bolan nodded his understanding. "Have the doctors told you how long you might have?" he asked.

Antangana shrugged. "A few weeks. Perhaps a few months. No two cases, they tell me, are quite the same." His words were becoming lower and more like growls than speech. The effort it took him to talk was obviously taking its toll. "I am due for another round of chemotherapy in a few days," he managed to choke out.

Bolan stood up next to the man. "With all due respect, Mr. Prime Minister," he said, "I think it's time for me to take charge."

Antangana nodded. Suddenly, he had run out of air completely and had to take in a deep, wheezy-sounding breath. Then, leaning low to speak into Bolan's ear, he whispered, "I love my country. Please. Save it."

Before Bolan could respond, Antangana had stumbled around him and taken the chair the soldier had previously occupied. Bolan watched him out of the corner of his eye. As he sat, the lapel of the man's suit jacket rode up around his ears, making him appear to shrink and look even thinner and more worn out than he'd appeared when he'd stood.

"Gentlemen," Bolan said as soon as the prime minister was seated. "A few of you I know, others I don't. But during this time of peril for Cameroon, we're all going to get to know each other as we go." He leaned forward and pressed the palms of his hands on the top of the table. "As I see it, we've got two missions here. To keep the candidates alive, and to find former president Robert Menye and either deliver him to the International Criminal Court or kill him."

"But what about the candidates?" the young soldier who had spoken earlier blurted out. "They are no better than Menye. Maybe worse. Why should we waste our time protecting them when either one would begin a genocide against the other's followers as soon as he took office?"

"Because with our presence in your country," Bolan said as he swept his hand along the line of chairs where the Secret Service men and Lareby sat, "the world will blame the United States for the assassination of either or both candidates. As to how to handle things once one of them is elected," he went on, "I can't answer that yet. Maybe NATO will send in peacekeeping troops until things stabilize. Maybe the International Criminal Court will sanction America to handle it. In any case, I can't afford to worry about that yet. We've got to take things one step at a time, and that means making sure both candidates stay alive."

"Pardon me, sir," an older black man in a gray suit said, "but it is unclear to me exactly who you are." He waited for an answer.

When he didn't get one, he said, "Perhaps I was the one who was unclear. We would be in your debt if you would tell us what American law-enforcement agencies or espionage bureaus you represent."

Bolan nodded. "The men in the dark suits are U.S. Secret

Service agents. Every one of them has protected our own President at one time or another, and they'll be split into teams to help cover the candidates." He cast a quick glance at Lareby whose head moved slightly side to side. This was not the kind of situation where the CIA would want to be outed. So he left it at that, hoping the Cameroonians would believe Lareby was also a Secret Service agent.

"And you?" the same elderly man asked the soldier.

Bolan reached into the inside pocket of his sports coat and pulled out a badge case. "United States Department of Justice," he said, holding up the phony credentials that identified him as Special Agent Matt Cooper. "My field of specialization is counterterrorism."

That seemed to satisfy the men around the table.

All except for the same elderly black man.

"Thank you," the man said. "But all but one of the men you have introduced are dressed in suits. Are we to believe that the gentleman in the khaki vest seated here is also Secret Service?" He paused a second, then added, "It is not just his clothing. There is something different about him. Something I cannot 'put my finger on' as you Americans sometimes say."

Before Bolan could speak, Dr. John Lareby began patting his vest down like an underage kid looking for a fake driver's license to buy beer. "Damn," he finally said, "I know I had my credentials when we took off from Washington." A sudden look of revelation combined with embarrassment fell over his face. "I must have left them in my carry-on on the plane."

"Then the ID card is in cinders and the badge has melted," one of the Secret Service men with a well-trimmed mustache said. Bolan could tell by his face that the man sensed Lareby was CIA, and was adding his own two cents to help cover the fact.

"I'm Secret Service, too," Lareby finally said. "I'm just not as fancy a dresser as the rest of these guys."

His remark brought another round of chuckles from around the table.

"Then we shall have to take your word for who you are," the gray-haired Cameroonian said. Bolan read his face just like he had Lareby's, and the thin smile told him that this man knew Lareby had to be with the Central Intelligence Agency. "I am sure when you are resupplied for the items you lost in the plane, a new badge and credentials will be included."

Lareby nodded. "I'll make sure of it," he said with a straight face.

Bolan found himself impressed with both men's performances. When working in any type of undercover capacity, it was the little things that counted. And although most of the Cameroonians obviously sensed that the Justice Department story for Bolan and Lareby's association with the Secret Service were lies, their faces still looked sincere as a tacit agreement to keep playing this game fell into place.

Sometimes, it was more important *not* to know something than it was to know it.

"I'll vouch for him until we can get duplicate credentials sent over," Bolan said. "He'll be working directly with me rather than being part of either of the candidate-protection details."

"Doing what, exactly, then?" the older man asked.

Bolan looked the man directly in the eye. "While the rest of the Secret Service looks after your candidates' protection, Dr. Lareby and I are going hunting."

"Hunting?" another young soldier almost screamed from farther down the table. "At a time like this, when all of Cameroon depends on what happens in the election, you two are planning on taking an African safari?"

He was interrupted by the older, gray-haired man. "They are not planning to shoot wildebeest and lions, my young friend," he said. "I believe what he meant was that they are going hunting for our former president."

Bolan's nod was slight, but everyone at the table caught it.

And understood what it meant.

3

The prime minister's staff had arranged for three suites to house the Americans. They were located on the third floor of the Hilton downtown, and would be used as a meeting place for the entire team; a location where both interviews and interrogations could be conducted, and a site for the Secret Service agents to "crash" when they weren't on duty.

Each of the two Cameroonian presidential candidates would have a pair of Secret Service agents by his side at all times. They would also be in charge of the Cameroon military protection agents who worked for Colonel Essam, and deal with the private bodyguards from within the two political parties.

As for Essam and his men, Bolan had assigned them to create an "outer circle" around the block on which the Hilton stood. They would be the first line of defense against perceived threats and, with luck, be able to end the problems before they got any closer to the men in the hotel.

Essam had not liked being so far away from the nucleus of the action, but Bolan had encountered his type before. It had taken only a few words to convince the colonel just how important the outer ring was before he puffed out his chest and agreed to the assignment.

As he shoved the key card into the door of suite 307, the Executioner wondered just how well it was all going to work. The colonel had left their brief encounter after the meeting with a smile. But the Executioner thought that smile had looked forced. It was clear that the colonel was more accustomed to giving orders than taking them, and Bolan wondered just how long it would be before his resentment overcame the thin flattery.

The light atop the lock turned green and Bolan twisted the doorknob open. His plan was a somewhat unconventional setup in regard to bodyguarding, or VIP protection, as it was commonly referred to these days. The U.S. Secret Service would be with the two presidential candidates in the suites and anywhere else they moved them, while Colonel Essam and his men ran a "roving guard" throughout the hotel's halls and lobby, as well as circling the Hilton in unmarked street vehicles.

Bolan wasn't crazy about the arrangement. It gave him no view of what Essam and his men were doing, and their abilities were a far cry from those of the expert Secret Service men. This meant the outer ring of protection was vulnerable to penetration, and assassination attempts that should have been seen and halted before they got anywhere near the two candidates might very well be executed.

But such was the game Bolan had walked into. And while his jurisdiction over the Secret Service and Lareby was a definite, it extended to the Cameroonian military only on paper. He had little doubt that if Essam contradicted his orders, the soldiers under him would obey their colonel.

The situation was "iffy" at best.

There was another aspect that troubled Bolan even more, and was constantly at the back of his mind. The enemy had known when his aircraft was landing, and how many men were getting off. And those two things spelled *traitor* to the

Executioner. He was going to have to keep his eyes on his own men as well as those of the CPU and KDNP.

Lareby followed the soldier into their separate suite next to that of the Secret Service and said, "Which bedroom do you want?"

Bolan scanned the area, then said, "I'll probably end up sleeping out here on the couch. If I get a chance to sleep at all. I want to keep one ear open for anything going on to our sides or in the hall."

Lareby nodded. "We'll probably hear Essam's lackeys pounding up and down the halls most of the time," he said. "But you think I should do the same? I could pull that other couch up near the door and—" he pointed across the room at a slightly shorter version of the sofa Bolan had indicated "—and I could rack out next to—"

The big American shook his head. "There's no need for both of us to do that," he said. "Besides, we're going to spend a lot more time away from this room than in it."

"Okay," the CIA man said and headed for the nearest bedroom.

Bolan walked to the phone on a nightstand next to the couch and lifted the receiver to his ear, at the same time pulling a business card out of his jacket pocket. A moment later he had punched in the number printed on the card, and a moment after that the hospital answered.

"Jack Grimaldi's room, please," Bolan said.

As he waited, he caught himself grinning. Grimaldi had awakened before the ambulance could arrive and, still under the influence of the morphine Lareby had administered, tried to get out of the jeep just as the meeting had broken up. He was raring to go after the men who had shot him, and it had been difficult to get him to go to the hospital. Just as the ambulance had arrived, Bolan had finally convinced him by saying, "Look, Jack. It doesn't hurt to be careful. Besides, you'll just be hanging around, waiting for our folks to send one of the other jets. Just do it for me, okay? I can't afford to use a pilot who isn't running at one hundred percent."

Even under the drug's influence, Grimaldi had seen through the ruse. But he had finally nodded in agreement.

The phone buzzed in Bolan's ear, and a second later he heard Grimaldi pick up the receiver next to his hospital bed. "It must be you, Sarge," the pilot growled. "Nobody else knows I'm here."

"Ease up, old buddy," he said. "Actually, everybody back home at the Farm knows where you are. I told them when I called for another plane to be sent over. How are you feeling?"

"I'm fine," Grimaldi said. "Got a few stitches is all. But they want to keep me overnight for observation. Frankly, it all makes me feel like something growing in a test tube. There's only one reason I haven't already walked out of here."

"And I'll just bet she has a name," the Executioner said with a chuckle.

"As a matter of fact, she does." Grimaldi laughed back. "Although I can't pronounce it. In any case, she's promised me a sponge bath as soon as her shift is over."

"You get well," Bolan came back. "There's no telling when we might need you."

"Affirmative, big guy," the pilot said.

In the background, Bolan heard what sounded like a hospital privacy curtain closing.

"Gotta go," Grimaldi said. "Got a visitor. And she's armed with a sponge."

The Executioner was still smirking as he hung up. But his momentary light spirit disappeared when he heard the sudden knock on the door to the hall. It came in the form of five strikes with little-to-no pauses in between.

It was *not* the two knocks, pause, and then two more raps that he and the Secret Service men had agreed upon as their "code knock" when visiting one anothers rooms.

From beneath his torn and battle-rumpled sports coat, the Executioner drew the sound-suppressed 9 mm Beretta 93-R.

Then he walked toward the peephole.

BOLAN HELD the 93-R in front of the peephole for a good three seconds before dropping the Beretta to his side. More than one man had been shot through a peephole when the gunman on the other side saw it darken, and the Executioner had no intention of joining that club. Finally satisfied that it wasn't a ruse, he stuck an eye in front of the hole.

A moment later, he opened the door. "What are you doing here?" the soldier asked bluntly. "You should be in bed. Or getting your chemotherapy."

A brief expression of sadness covered Antangana's face. Then it switched almost magically into a knowing grin. "I do not restart my treatments for another couple of days," he said. "So I thought I would come to assist you."

Bolan opened the door wider and let the man into the room.

The soldier had barely recognized Antangana. The man had changed out of his suit into a pair of worn brown slacks, sandals and a brightly colored dashiki. The loose garment—like the suit coat before it—seemed to emphasize his emaciation.

"I was President Menye's prime minister," the man said as soon as Bolan had swung the door closed and replaced the Beretta in his shoulder rig. "And no one knows that evil man better than I do. I will help you find him, and I will help you kill him." His grin seemed to take up all of his face, and

Bolan saw a perfect row of gleaming white teeth behind his upper lip.

Bolan looked the man up and down. He was still getting into this mission, and the one thing he'd learned so far was that he couldn't be certain who could be trusted and who could not. Antangana's multicolored African-patterned dashiki was so large on him it could have hidden any number of weapons.

"Don't take this personally," the soldier said as he reached out, twisted the man to face away from him and patted him down. The closest thing to a weapon he found was an Okapi folding knife in the man's right front pocket. Opening the folding blade, he looked down at the inexpensive steel. Patterned loosely after the centuries-renowned Spanish *navajas,* the Okapis were manufactured in South Africa and although nonlocking and difficult to sharpen, they could be deadly in the hand of a man who knew how to use them.

Antangana's knife didn't look as if it had been used for much more than peeling apples or cutting vegetables. Bolan folded the knife closed again and dropped it in his pocket for the time being.

"With all due respect, Mr. Prime Minister," the soldier asked, "exactly what is it you think you can do to help, considering your health?"

"I know this country," Antangana stated. "I know it as well as I know myself. And I know the people and our customs. I can help you deal with them without accidentally offending them and turning them to stone." He paused to catch his breath. "I believe you Americans say something like I can 'cut through the bullshit.'"

Bolan had to fight to keep a smile from forming on his own face. "Well," he said, "have a seat." Unleathering the Beretta again and gesturing with it at the couch.

Antangana dropped down on the couch as Bolan took a

padded armchair. A second later, Lareby came out of the bedroom. The CIA man had taken off his vest and rolled the sleeves of his shirt up to his elbows. He was drying his hands with a white towel as he crossed the threshold. "I see we have company," he said.

Bolan kept his eyes on the man in the dashiki. "Yes, we do," he said. "You remember him, I'm sure. Antangana—Jean—Antangana. Unfortunately at this point, he belongs to the group of men I trust the *least* in the world."

"Oh, yeah?" Lareby said as he finished drying his hands and arms. "And what group might that be?"

"Volunteer informants," the Executioner replied. "They're almost always playing both ends against the middle."

By this point, Antangana had bent one knee beneath him and was sitting on his own foot while his other leg extended to the floor. In spite of Bolan's words, the smile he had entered the room wearing never left his face. "I understand your logic," he said. "And I must admit I would probably distrust you if our roles were reversed. But I promise you I am an exception. So. What can I do to gain your confidence?"

"You can start by telling us why you didn't volunteer your help earlier at the meeting."

"Because there were men present who *I* do not trust," Antangana said simply. "And I did not want them to know any more about your plans than necessary."

The man's sickly appearance seemed to loom even larger as he tried to take a deep breath. There was something about him—something Bolan couldn't put his finger on—that made the Executioner believe he was sincere in his desire to assist them. "Who don't you trust?" he asked.

"There are several I suspect of sympathizing with the KDNP. Others with the CPU. And one or two, I am relatively certain, are still loyal to President Menye."

Bolan thought about the man's words for a moment. His

gut still told him that this man was telling the truth. It would be difficult, if not impossible, to grow up in a country such as Cameroon without taking on prejudices of one sort or another. While the remaining leaders of the nation might not be actual members of the KDNP or CPU, they would likely lean one way or the other.

"Assuming I believe you," Bolan finally said. "What would make you want to help us at this time? Particularly since you were one of Menye's top men before he vacated his little throne." The Executioner rarely used sarcasm, but when he did, it cut all the way to the bone.

Antangana shrugged. "The answer to your question is really not very complicated," he said. "When he first took office, Menye was not the self-inflated potentate that he gradually became. I was proud to work for him then. But, little by little, he began to change. A small lie here. An execution carried out for personal reasons there. Before long, he had created a regime far more remorselessly cruel than Cameroon had ever known in the past." Antangana paused and drew in another deep breath. "And so I was stuck."

"You tried to resign?" Bolan asked.

"I did," Antangana said. "I do not remember Menye's exact words, but they included that my head might look attractive on top of a spear stuck into the ground." He paused and traded legs beneath him. "That dampened my enthusiasm for resigning rather quickly."

Lareby had pulled one of the chairs away from the dining-room table, flipped it backward, then sat with his arms crossed over the back, his chin resting on them. "I can see how it might," the CIA man said. "But why didn't you just leave the country and seek asylum in America or somewhere else?"

"Because by the time I realized how power-crazed he had become," Antangana said, staring hard at the man, "too much had already occurred. I was afraid any country in which I sought refuge would consider me as guilty as Menye himself. Besides, the man had already murdered two of his staff who he only *suspected* of plotting against him. I had no desire to be the third."

Lareby and Bolan exchanged glances and nods. The story sounded believable. The soldier turned back to Antangana. "All right," he said, standing up. "I'm going to give you a shot. And you can take that statement both literally and figuratively. If you're on the level and really want to help us, great. But if it turns out that you have your own personal agenda that conflicts with ours, all I can promise you is a faster and more humane death than your old boss would have given you." He reholstered the Beretta and pulled the Okapi out of his pocket, flipping it across the room to Antangana. "Try to use that piece of steel on me or anyone else, and I'll kill you with it," he said. "Understood?"

"Quite well," the prime minister said. "And please believe me when I tell you I have no hidden agenda of any sort. My only goals are to save my country and pray that my chemotherapy is successful. If I cannot be successful with the second goal, I hope to see my country become a peaceful democracy before I die. And, oh, yes…I want to see Menye caught or killed, of course."

Bolan and Lareby remained silent.

"May I assume, then," Antangana said after another breath, "that we are all in agreement?" He rocked forward and came back to his feet, pulling the leg on which he sat out from the couch and returning it to the floor.

Bolan nodded. "We'll try to take Menye alive so his war crimes can be exposed to the rest of the world. But I can't promise you that'll be possible," he said.

"It is possible that if he is tried in the International Criminal Court that he might go free," Antangana said, and for the first time since he'd entered the room his smile became a frown. "One never knows what can happen during a trial. Evidence can become tainted and thrown out. The truth can be twisted." A few beads of sweat had broken out on his forehead. "Menye is the most guilty man I have ever known," he said as he wiped his face with the sleeve of the dashiki. "He has sacked this nation worse than Genghis Khan or Attila the Hun ever dreamed about, using embezzlement, nationalization of the oil, timber and coffee industries, and outright murder to funnel millions of dollars into his bank accounts in Switzerland and the Cayman Islands." He fell silent for a moment and closed his eyes. "But still, it is quite possible that he could walk free."

"Maybe," Bolan said. "But it didn't work that way for Saddam Hussein." He turned and jerked his bullet-ridden sports coat from the back of the chair. One shoulder was still ripped out but until more equipment, clothing and supplies arrived from America, it would have to do as a cover for his Beretta and Desert Eagle.

"But if the worst should happen and he is found not guilty..." Antangana stared at the big man across the room, letting the sentence trail off unfinished. But the quiver in his voice betrayed his terror at the possibility that Menye might once again take the reins of power in Cameroon.

"Then I'll personally carry out the execution," Bolan said, as he stuck his arms into his jacket.

Since he was going by the name Matt Cooper, neither of the other two men in the room caught the double meaning in the Executioner's last statement. "Is there anything else you've got to tell us?" Bolan asked.

"I know where Menye is hiding," he said simply.

Bolan stopped with one arm in the jacket, the other still out. He had begun to expect some good intel from this new informant, but not a bombshell like this. The soldier had to remind himself that Antangana's story still needed to be confirmed. If the man was playing double agent, it could all be a trap.

Lareby was less diplomatic about his suspicions. "How do you know where he is if you're not still in league with him?" the CIA man asked gruffly.

"In Cameroon there are very few secrets," Antangana said. "Although Menye's location is one of them."

"Get to the point," Bolan said as he finished shrugging into his jacket and sat back against the chair.

"I have an informant of my own who saw suspicious men entering through the alley door of an old abandoned warehouse," the prime minister said. "He recognized one of Menye's personal bodyguards who had disappeared when Menye took off." He frowned a moment. "I believe you Americans call it 'going away with sheep?'"

Lareby suppressed a laugh. "Close. It's called 'going on the lamb.'"

Bolan looked across the room, through the window, and saw that dusk was falling over Yaounde. "Yeah," he said. "It means he's running."

"Where does it come from?" Antangana asked, frowning. "I know of no lambs that—"

The Executioner was growing impatient with this man who was obviously easily sidetracked. "I don't know where it comes from and it doesn't matter. You have an address for this warehouse location?"

"I do," Antangana said. "But it is in the most dangerous slum in Yaounde. Murders occur every night."

"That doesn't matter." Bolan rose from his chair. He had relied on his Desert Eagle during the gun battle back at the airport, and was down to one full magazine and one partially loaded with five shots. Until his supplies arrived, he would have to make do with what he had. He patted the Beretta

beneath his jacket. It was still filled with 9 mm fragmentation rounds, and he had two extra magazines under his right
arm opposite the pistol in his shoulder holster.

It might be enough. Or it might not. In any case, he would
be sure to pick up the weapons of his enemies as he went.

Looking quickly across the room, he saw Lareby checking his own weapon. "How are you fixed?" Bolan asked.

"Full gun, one extra mag," the CIA man said.

Bolan knew the small double action .380 held eight
rounds, with one in the chamber. The other magazine would
give Lareby an additional seven. "Better make them count
then," he said.

The CIA counterterrorist expert nodded.

The soldier took another glance outside and saw that darkness was replacing the twilight he had seen a few moments
earlier. Antangana had held the closed Okapi folding knife
in his fist ever since Bolan tossed it back to him, but now he
watched the man drop it back into the same pocket where it
had been found during the search.

"Let's go," Antangana said simply, then led the men out
the door, into the elevator and out of the hotel into the night.

4

The strong odor of trash and human waste nearly blocked out the smell of the other odors in Yaounde's darkened business district. The area was half-deserted. Bolan watched through the back window of the taxicab and saw gangs of young men walking up and down the streets. The teenagers were doing their best to look and act like American gangbangers, and wore an almost laughable combination of Western attire—baseball caps turned backward, and sleeveless T-shirts that emphasized elaborate tattoos—mixed with dashikis and other African attire. He remembered the cabdriver asking if this was *really* the part of town they wanted to visit. Bolan had said simply, "Yes."

He continued to use all of his senses as he took in the atmosphere of this neighborhood. Barely present above the nauseous odors was the scent of oil, freshly cut pine and other woods, and coffee beans. But he saw no one on the streets who looked like they worked in any of those enterprises.

The workmen, he suspected, scuttled out as soon as closing time came each day, giving way to the human "vampires" who ruled the night. He remembered what Jean Antangana had said earlier, back at the hotel, about this being the most dangerous area of the city. And although the Executioner had seen even more poverty and crime in places like Calcutta and the fish market area of Iquitos, Peru, he sensed that violence could break out at any time.

Like in most Third World countries, tourists were forbidden to bear weapons, and their clothing and the large sums of money they likely carried made them easy targets. Bolan knew that while he—with the ripped shoulder and torn lapel of his coat—didn't look like the typical tourist, the semiruined jacket could be misinterpreted as the result of an earlier mugging.

Lareby's multipocketed vest, faded blue jeans and Timberland hiking boots shouted "Visitor," and even Antangana, with his expensive dashiki and carefully pressed slacks, looked out of place.

The soldier glanced at the scrap of paper Antangana had given him. The address of the warehouse where Menye and the men still loyal to him were supposedly hiding was accompanied by a crude, hand-drawn map of the area.

Bolan looked up at a street sign as they passed. Unless he had misinterpreted the map, they were roughly three blocks away from the address he had given the cabbie. Not wanting the driver to know their exact location lest he alert one or more of the roving gangsters of the "easy pickings," he had told the man to drop him off two blocks before they reached the warehouse in question.

This was Yaounde—the capital city of a nation in tremendous upheaval.

And Bolan didn't trust *anyone*.

The cabdriver finally pulled to a halt and Bolan leaned forward, handing him several Communauté Financière Africaine franc bills. He added several more to what would have been a normal tip, and said, "You never saw us. Right?"

"Right," the cabbie said, smiling. But then his smile turned quickly to a frown. "One last time, my friends. Are you *sure* this is where you desire to be let out?" He paused for a second, then started to speak again before Bolan could answer. "I could take you to a very fine brothel in a safer part of the city. The women are all beautiful, and—"

Bolan interrupted with, "No thanks," as he shut the door behind him. He stood silently as the cab drove quickly away. It was obvious that the driver didn't care to spend any more time in this neighborhood than he had to.

Antangana stepped up next to Bolan. "According to my informant, there is a rear exit that Menye's men use. Menye, of course, does not leave at all. He is too easily recognized. I suggest we follow the alleys, then make our entrance into the building in the same way."

Bolan nodded. "You were the prime minister, right?" he asked.

"Yes."

"Then why is it that the only thing even resembling a weapon you have is that cheap Okapi?" Bolan asked. "I remember seeing pictures of Menye and some of his other cabinet members. They were always in uniform and always armed."

"I am not a fighter," Antangana said. "I am a strategist."

"Then strategize from a point about ten feet behind us," Bolan said as he led the way down a darkened alley. "And don't get in our way if trouble breaks out."

Antangana nodded.

But trouble came even before the three men were expecting it.

THE FIRST THING Bolan saw as they entered the alley was the beam of a flashlight, aimed directly into his eyes. For a second, he was blinded. Then he closed his eyelids as quickly as he could. He knew the light had shifted when he felt the heat of the strong beam leave his face, and when he opened his eyes again he could see only blurry forms of Lareby and Antangana. Their eyes had been forced closed as well.

Bolan grimaced. He knew that they'd all lose their night vision for several minutes.

Turning back to the oncoming light, the Executioner saw the distinctive outline of a large halogen torchlight. It contained both a huge spotlight-style plastic beam, which was the one being used on them, and a softer, more regular flashlight mounted on the top. Holding the heated beam, Bolan could make out the dark and fuzzy form of a man wearing his baseball cap backward. A dashiki rivaling Antangana's in flashy color fell halfway down his thighs.

To his sides and behind him, Bolan saw other barely visible forms in the darkness. He counted a total of six in addition to the torchbearer, and knew they were another of the roving night gangs he'd seen since entering the slum.

For a moment no one spoke, and Bolan used the time to close his eyes tightly once again. His quick reaction to the light had limited his loss of night vision. When he glanced toward Lareby, he saw that the CIA man was regaining his sight, too.

But Antangana had taken the full beam directly in the face, which meant a good fifteen to thirty minutes before the "strategist" regained his ability to see in the dark.

When he lifted his eyelids once more, Bolan's vision was almost back to normal. Apparently the instrument had done its job in the opinion of the man holding it, since he had dropped the beam to the ground. But the light was still so strong that it lit the immediate area around the two parties.

The Executioner's eyes skirted from the torchbearer to each of the other six men. He saw baseball bats in the hands of two of the men. A third had a crowbar, and the other three held knives of various sizes and shapes. As he turned his attention back to the man who'd held the powerful light, he saw him reaching up under the dashiki. He produced a Kiribati—a light wooden stick with shark's teeth bound to the edges. It had originated in the Gilbert Islands centuries earlier, and had been a step away from the club toward the sword.

How it had wound up in the hands of a Cameroonian gangbanger was anybody's guess. But just as it had destroyed human flesh hundreds of years ago, it was capable of doing the same now.

So far, no one had spoken, and Bolan's mind quickly returned to the limited supply of ammo his men had. They couldn't afford wasting valuable rounds on these street punks when they were almost sure to go up against automatic weapons when they arrived at the warehouse to search for Menye.

Bolan finally broke the silence with a simple "What is it you want, boys?"

"Ah," the leader said in a heavy North African accent. "You speak English."

"How very perceptive of you," Lareby said sarcastically.

"Then you are Englishmen?" the leader asked.

"American," Bolan corrected him. He glanced over his shoulder to Antangana and saw the prime minister rubbing his eyes. Antangana—admittedly a noncombatant—was going to be of no use at all when the fight started in a minute.

"Americans?" the gang leader said. "Wonderful! I love to kill Americans." His laugh came as much through his nose as his mouth, and sounded more like the snort of a pig than a human.

"But I like some of your clothes," the man who'd held the giant flashlight went on. "Perhaps if you give us all of your clothing and all of your money, who knows? We might let you live."

Bolan turned toward Lareby at his side. "Remember our limited ammunition," he whispered.

Lareby nodded. He already had his hand inside his vest and appeared to be holding on to something.

Bolan reached behind him to the Tactical Operations Loner knife lodged in the Kydex sheath and clipped to his belt. It was not a big knife as edged weapons went—only 4.5 inches in blade length. But the blade was wide, and in addition to the primary edge, the back edge was sharpened to a diamond-shaped reinforced tip that not only strengthened the point but further opened a slash wound that originated farther back toward the grip.

A second later, the Executioner had drawn it and held it low at his side, but with the tip pointed toward the gang leader's eyes. It was a technique all trained knife fighters knew, which made it harder for the knife to be seen. Especially in the semilight of the alley.

"Then you choose to die?" the gangbanger asked.

"Funny thing," Bolan said. "I was just thinking the same thing about you."

The gangster looked around him. "The man behind you does not look as if he will be of much help," he said. An evil-looking smile began to curl his lips upward. "We are seven. You are two. *Maybe* three. This will not be a very fair fight."

"You're right," the Executioner said. "You'd better go get some more guys."

The words angered the gang leader and he sprang suddenly forward, swinging the Kiribati toward his adversary's head in an overhead motion.

With the stealth and speed of a snake, Bolan lifted the Loner and cut the man's wrist as it descended. He checked the blow with his left hand, slapping the gangbanger's forearm slightly to the side.

The ancient weapon missed Bolan's shoulder by less than an inch. But it wasn't horseshoes they were playing, and "close" didn't count. In a knife fight an inch was as good as twenty miles.

The gang leader screamed. Dropping his short club, he pulled his arm into his chest and shrieked, "Kill them!"

The other six men moved forward, their weapons raised. In his peripheral vision, Bolan could see that Lareby had produced a Laci Szabo-designed miniature bowie knife. With a blade that measured out at a little over six inches, it had a radically curved maplewood handle that made it both fast in the hand and almost impossible to drop or have taken away.

A gangster wearing a filthy white T-shirt, equally dirty athletic shoes, and a small snap-brimmed hat moved in toward the Executioner. Bolan waited until he was in range and let him bring his baseball bat high over his head. At just the right moment—before the bat could begin its descent—the soldier stepped in and slashed the man's triceps.

The bat fell from the gangbanger's hand, directly onto his shoulder, then rolled off his back to hit the ground behind him. Without the use of his triceps—the muscle that held the arm outright—the thug's hand dropped impotently to his side.

The Executioner grabbed the dreadlocks that shot out from all sides of the small hat, and he jerked the man's face backward to expose his throat. The rear edge of the Loner sliced back through the throat, the diamond-shaped tip widening the wound like the weird, giant smile of a circus clown.

It was a smile of death, and Bolan pushed the man away from him as the gangster bled out on his way to the ground.

Next to him, Lareby was putting his small bowie-style knife to good use. One of the young men—holding the wickedly curved blade of a kris—lunged forward with a thrust. Bolan's fellow American stepped slightly to the side, twisted the Szabo knife in his hand and brought it down in a vicious backcut across his opponent's forearm.

The thrust of the kris shot past him as he moved, and Lareby twisted the blade again, swinging a reverse backcut across the man's forehead just above the eyebrows. The sudden gush of blood that fell into the man's eyes left him blinded. And although he held on to the dagger, he let his arm fall to his side just as his compatriot had.

Bolan glanced into his blood-filled eyes. The man had a confused look about him, as if his brain had not yet registered exactly what had happened.

But he also looked like a man who had resigned himself to death.

And death he got. As Bolan prepared to face the next man, Lareby finished off his attacker with a hilt-deep thrust into the heart. When the blade had finally stopped at the guard, Lareby pumped it up and down several times. What blood had not yet sprung from the other wounds to his body now shot out directly from the chest wound as Lareby quickly spun away to get out of its path.

The next street punk had silver rings hanging from both ears, both nostrils and his bottom lip. They were all connected by silver chains that hung loosely on the man's face. Designed to frighten people, it did nothing for Bolan as he reached out and grabbed the chain on the right side of the man's face. A sharp tug tore the ear, nose and lip rings from his face. The chain followed, bringing with it part of the man's ear, nostril and the entire right side of his lip.

The scream that echoed down the alley could have come from a gutted pig.

But it didn't last long. Bolan twirled the Loner into a reverse grip, brought it up, then down just above the other man's collarbone. The wide blade severed the subclavian artery, and crimson fluid shot up and out of his neck like a fountain. The Executioner let him drop where he stood.

A quick glance toward Antangana told Bolan the man was still having trouble seeing. But he had drawn the Okapi from his pocket, opened it and was slashing back and forth in front of him.

And hoping the last man with a knife heading his way would be fended off.

Bolan knew his effort would be in vain. The last blade looked like a crudely made, spear-pointed throwing knife that had been sharpened on both sides. What little light there was in the alley gleamed off its edges, and he could see that the grip had been wrapped in silver duct tape.

The knife might be crude, but it could kill just as easily as a thousand-dollar custom blade.

The last gangbanger stopped just out of the range of the Okapi, and Bolan saw that he was timing Antangana's back-and-forth slashes. Cameroon's prime minister didn't even know enough about what he was doing to vary the speed or angles. In another second or two, the man with the sharpened throwing knife would dart in, and Antangana would pay for his lack of knowledge with his life.

Bolan turned, seeing that Lareby was playing a game of cat and mouse with the last man who carried one of the base-ball bats. This thug knew what he was doing better than his friends, and he had shifted his hands with one gripping the barrel of the bat and the other on the handle. Such a grip shortened the range of an "extension" weapon like a bat, but it multiplied its fast manipulation a hundredfold.

The man with the "souped up" throwing knife had already

taken a step in when Bolan lunged toward his back. As he collided with him, the soldier raised the Loner slightly over his head, then brought it down toward his opponent's back. But the collision had thrown him slightly off balance, and the blade dug through the man's skin just below the heart into the aorta.

The effect was practically the same.

Just to make sure, Bolan reached around the man and grabbed his face with his left hand. In what looked like one smooth movement, he extracted the wide blade from the gangbanger's back, brought it around to the front of the man's neck and sliced through both the internal and external jugular veins.

Antangana had instinctively stepped back from the action, and the man with the throwing blade hit the ground face-first at his feet.

Bolan turned, never knowing what the gangster he had just killed even looked like.

The only enemy still standing was the man going one-on-one with Lareby. The CIA agent had taken a modified saber-fencing stance, and was moving back and forth, staying just out of range of the longer bat. Bolan could see red liquid dripping from the hand on the barrel of the bat, and that told him that Lareby had already gotten at least one cut or thrust into the man's fingers. But it had missed the tendons and ligaments, thereby allowing him to continue holding the bat.

Lareby was obviously well-trained in the process of what Filipino martial artists called "defanging the snake." His plan was to cut the closest targets—the hands—until the bat fell to the ground. Then the CIA man would move in for the kill.

But Bolan's next glance showed red marks on Lareby's

face, which would turn black and blue by tomorrow. The gangbanger was holding his own. As Bolan watched, the punk suddenly struck with the middle of the bat under Lareby's chin. The blow knocked the CIA man's head up and back, and the soldier could almost hear the man's teeth rattle inside his head. A split second later, the gangbanger switched his grip to a more traditional baseball bat hold.

Bolan saw it coming. The last street punk turned slightly, and the Executioner saw that he wore a Hard Rock Café T-shirt. The big American wondered, briefly, whether the shirt had been donated to some charity and shipped overseas, or whether it was a local knock-off. No matter. As the Executioner started toward him, the man prepared to swing the bat at Lareby's head.

If it struck his temple, Lareby's head would smash like a watermelon with a stick of dynamite inserted into it. Or if the swing was meant for the CIA man's throat, it would crush the common carotid and vertebral arteries.

If that didn't kill him on the spot, it would leave the agent a paraplegic for life.

As Bolan moved closer, he knew he was still too far away to stop it.

With the Loner still in his right hand, the Executioner curved his left wrist back under his arm and drew the sound-suppressed Beretta. With no time to look for the sights, he flipped the selector switch to semiauto and point-aimed the weapon at the gangster's head. A near-silent round struck the man holding the bat in the temple, blowing blood and brain matter out of both entry and exit holes.

The last gangbanger fell in a heap on the dirty alley ground.

A look of relief came over Lareby's face as he turned to face Bolan. "It's just like they say," he said. "I saw my life flash before my eyes." He reached up to rub his chin. "Thanks."

"Don't mention it," the soldier said as he holstered the Beretta. "We're here to help each other."

"Well, then," Lareby said with a smile, "thanks for breaking your own rule about not using any ammunition."

"I never said don't use any ammunition," Bolan said. "I said we needed to *conserve* it."

"Right," Lareby said, nodding. "I guess one bullet and six dead isn't too much of an expenditure."

"I can live with it," Bolan said. "Both literally and figuratively."

Antangana had walked up to the two men while they were talking, and he said, "I am ashamed. I was of no use at all."

Bolan shook his head. "You've got nothing to apologize for," he said. "It was your intel that got us this far."

The Executioner's words didn't seem to salve the man's conscience or ego. "Thank you both anyway," he said. "Without you, I would be dead."

"Without us, you wouldn't even have been here," Bolan corrected. "You'd be safe at home and probably asleep right now."

"Perhaps," said Antangana. "But I am still ashamed of myself."

"For what?" Lareby asked, frowning.

"That I was not of any help in the fight."

"God made all kinds of people," Bolan said. "Not all of them are supposed to be warriors."

"Still," Antangana said. "Sometimes I wish I had been born a more righteously violent man like you are."

Bolan looked down at the shorter man. "I'm not a violent man," he said. "I just happen to be good at it when it's needed."

Antangana frowned for a moment, then his face relaxed as he understood what the Executioner's words had meant.

"Now," Bolan said. "Let's get on down the alley. To the *real* fight."

5

Silence fell over the odd trio of men as they made their way down the alley, crossing the side streets they encountered as they went. Bolan thought to himself that one of his skintight stretch battle garments, known as blacksuits, would have come in handy right about then. But the three he had stored on board the aircraft had all fallen to the fire, and no amount of wishful thinking was going to magically make one reassemble itself from the ashes. So as the Executioner always did, he would deal with the situation as it was.

Sometimes you just had to go with what you had.

And this was one of those times.

The Executioner remembered the single 9 mm round with which he'd killed the last gangbanger. The magazine had automatically chambered the next round, and he still had fourteen left in the Beretta's magazine, plus the ammo still left for the .44 Magnum Desert Eagle.

He'd have liked to have had more rounds—a rifle or shotgun, too—but wishing for them was just as big a waste of time as thinking about the blacksuit.

The party slowed as it reached the block where the abandoned warehouse was supposed to be. Reaching out with both hands, Bolan stopped the two men flanking him. "I'll take the lead. But I want you," he whispered as he looked toward Antangana, "to stay at the rear. There are a lot of back doors on this block. Can I assume your informant told you exactly which one it was?"

The prime minister nodded. "You may," he said. But Bolan noticed that he was shivering all over as the words came out of his mouth.

The three men walked on, carefully avoiding smashed tin cans, broken bottles and other debris that would make noise if stepped upon. Finally, Bolan felt a hand reach out from behind him and grasp his arm. Antangana nodded toward a dull gray steel door just ahead. In the moonlight, a combination padlock was barely visible next to the knob.

"Stay back," Bolan told the two men. In the semilight he saw both heads bob. Antangana and Lareby stopped in their tracks.

"Your snitch didn't happen to have the combination, did he?" Bolan asked Antangana.

The man shook his head.

"Then I'm going to have to shoot it off." Bolan stepped up to the door, his eyebrows lowered in thought as he drew the Beretta once more. The padlock meant that someone had locked the warehouse from the outside. Did that mean that Menye and his men had vacated the site during the time between Antangana learning of their location and the trio's arrival?

Maybe. Maybe not. It took only one man to lock up from the outside. There could still be gunmen loyal to the ex-president holed up inside. And it would only make sense that Menye would send at least one man back out "into the world" each day in order to pick up on the latest happenings and political climate in Cameroon.

Taking up a position against the door, the Executioner let the sound suppressor on the end of the 9 mm pistol press against the dial on the lock. Gently, he pulled the trigger and heard the gun emit a discreet cough. But when he reached out and tried to jerk the padlock open, he found that it had jammed.

Another wasted round in his limited supply of ammo.

Bolan pointed the Beretta at the dial again and sent another quiet round into the face of the lock. But the second attempt to jerk the lock open proved just as useless.

He turned back to Antangana and Lareby and whispered once more. "I'm going to have to shoot through the bar itself. Stand back again. The rounds will ricochet."

Reaching under his left arm, Bolan unsnapped one of the magazine carriers and withdrew a box mag of all-steel, pointed armor-piercing rounds—a type of ammo that had been outlawed because it could penetrate a ballistic nylon vest.

Bolan ejected the magazine from the butt of the Beretta, then turned the gun on its side and pulled the slide back to flip the fragmentation round up and out of the chamber. The slide automatically locked open, and the brass case gleamed upward into the moonlight.

The Executioner caught the round while it was still in the air.

Shoving the RBCD round back into the magazine from which it had come, he slid the box back into the carrier under his right arm. Then he inserted the armor-piercing mag into the butt of the Beretta and let the slide fly forward, chambering the first pointed round. Pressing the sound suppressor against one side of the U formed by the lock, he pulled the trigger once more.

As the Beretta coughed, something hit Bolan in the chest. When he looked down, he could see that a chip had been taken out of the bar. He tried the lock yet again.

But it was still no good.

Things simply weren't going his way on this night. At least not with the padlock.

Bolan took a deep breath. reminding himself that sometimes it was the little things a warrior encountered during a mission which determined victory or failure. Even though he was working as quietly as he could, he was still making some noise and he had to wonder if the men inside the warehouse—assuming there *were* men inside—might not be listening. He pressed his ear to the door. If they were listening, then they were waiting, too. Had they heard the soft cough of the sound suppressor? Had they listened to the bang of the padlock when it rocked back and forth against the steel door and frame?

Were they waiting inside, rifles pointed toward the door, ready to mow down whoever they thought it might be as soon as the door opened?

There was no way of knowing. Bolan heard nothing from inside the warehouse to indicate whether the enemy had taken notice of his attempts to enter.

Which meant little. The place might be deserted. Or perhaps the men inside had not paid any attention to the noises, or even heard them. On the other hand, they might also be expecting the return of the man who had locked the door from the outside.

The possibilities were too numerous to even fathom.

One of the possibilities—and the one for which Bolan had to prepare—was that the former Cameroonian president's men had heard every squeak and screech of metal-on-metal, determined exactly what it meant and were armed and ready.

As the old saying went, Hope for the best, but prepare for the worst.

But regardless of the enemies' state of readiness, time had now become a factor, and that superseded stealth.

For a second, Bolan considered pulling the mammoth Desert Eagle from his hip holster and loading it with armor-piercing rounds as he had the Beretta. The big .44 Magnum round would tear the lock to pieces, but it would also announce their presence loud and clear.

The .44 was out. At least until the soldier knew for sure that they'd been discovered.

Closing his eyes against more flying chips of steel, Bolan switched the Beretta's selector to 3-round burst and held it against the lock. Three quiet burps came from the end of the suppressor, and tiny, sharp shreds of steel blew back into his face and neck. When he raised his eyelids once more, he saw that the lock was finally hanging open.

The three rounds in roughly the same spot on the lock bar had done the trick. But in killing the last street punk who had attacked Lareby with the baseball bat and destroying the lock, he had used up almost half of one of the three 9 mm magazines he carried.

He and Lareby would definitely have to rearm themselves with the enemies' weapons at the first opportunity.

Quietly, Bolan reached out, pulled the destroyed padlock from its hinge and set it on the cracked pavement behind him. He then twisted the doorknob.

But it was locked, too—from the inside—and there was no keyhole in the door, which meant it had to have been secured from the other side.

Okay, the Executioner thought, nothing but one more simple step that he hadn't counted on. And with it came some important intelligence.

Someone *was* inside the warehouse. He supposed that they could have locked the door from the inside, then left through the front door or one of the windows. But that was highly unlikely. Antangana's informant had seen them using this back door, and they would want to avoid being spotted on the street. But there was no way of knowing for sure until he got inside himself.

There was also no way he was going to be able to blow open the dead-bolt lock with 9 mm bullets. Not even the armor-piercing rounds.

Bolan stepped back and pulled a small flashlight from the inside pocket of his ripped sports coat. He was thankful that he'd had it on his person rather than with the other gear that had been destroyed in the jet. But before he turned the powerful beam on the door, he whispered once more to his men. "It's locked from the inside, too. So we can assume that somebody's in there. These 9s will take forever to bust the dead bolt. I'm going to have to use the .44, which means they'll know where we are before we even get inside."

Lareby already had his .380-caliber pistol in his hand. He nodded his approval.

Bolan turned toward the prime minister and said, "You stay back, Jean. Preferably outside here in the alley."

"If you will give me one of your guns," Antangana said in a quavering voice, "I will be happy to—"

"No," Bolan interrupted. "You won't. There are all kinds of ways to fight wars. You're a diplomat, my friend, and this country is going to need men like you when the dust settles. But in the meantime, this is a job for soldiers. And Lareby and I are soldiers." The Executioner continued to stare into the man's dark brown eyes as he said, "I'm sorry to be so blunt, but we don't have time for courtesies."

"I understand," Antangana said, taking a step back, and Bolan's estimation of the man rocketed upward. Jean Antangana wanted to be part of turning Cameroon into a functional nation, and had been willing to risk his own life to achieve that end. But he was wise enough to listen to his brain rather than his heart. And that brain told him he'd be more burden than help in what was inevitably going to be one giant shootout.

Bolan stuck the Beretta back into his shoulder holster, then drew the Desert Eagle. Quickly, he switched magazines much as he'd done with the 9 mm pistol. One pointed armor-piercing round—two at the most—would get the job done and tear the steel away from the lock.

What would happen after that was anybody's guess.

As Bolan turned toward Lareby, a drop of water hit his cheek. The alley had grown darker as a cloud passed over the moon, and the Executioner looked up to see that the sky was turning almost black with clouds that threatened to burst at any second.

"Looks like we're in for a little rain," Bolan said.

Lareby smiled. "And to pervert the old saying, 'We don't have enough sense to stay out *in* it.'"

"You ready?" Bolan asked.

Lareby nodded, holding up his Walther. "This reminds me of the 'Lady or the Tiger' story by O. Henry."

"Except that there's not likely to be many ladies inside," Bolan came back. "And it's a whole lot of tigers behind this door."

The soldier glanced again at the small Walther PPK in Lareby's hand. "I know you CIA boys love those little .380s," he said, "but you need to pick up something with a little more punch as soon as you can. Maybe inside here."

Lareby nodded again.

Bolan turned back to the warehouse, finally switching on the flashlight. He directed the beam toward the door—just long enough to see where the dead-bolt lock was located, then pushed the button to turn the light off again. But even that quick flash of light was enough to tell Bolan more about their situation. The door and frame looked practically new, which suggested that organized men had been at work on it recently. The men inside were concerned enough about security to install a new, all-steel door and frame, and lock the door both inside and out.

But the situation was about to change in other ways, too. The explosions from the big Desert Eagle would be heard over a large area. Then speed and power, rather than a clandestine approach, would become the name of the game.

Someone, or more likely *someones,* were hiding inside. And these *someones* would not only outnumber Bolan and Lareby, they'd outgun them as well.

And as soon as the first blast came from the big .44, they wouldn't even have surprise on their side.

For most warriors, it would have been a death trap.

But the Executioner was not most warriors.

Pressing the muzzle of the Desert Eagle against the narrow crack between the steel door and its frame, Bolan pulled the trigger.

And the big .44 Magnum roared.

6

Dennis McNiel could hardly even remember when he hadn't been a Secret Service agent. There were vague pictures in his brain of being an All-State high-school football player, the first crush he'd ever had on a girl and a failed marriage. But it all seemed so long ago, as if part of someone else's life.

McNiel took a seat on the couch in the living room of suite 309. It connected to 307, where the mysterious big man who called himself a Justice Department agent and the man McNiel had pegged as CIA through-and-through were staying. Suite 307, in turn, had an adjoining door to 305, which was where the other half of the Secret Service team would be "racking out" when not on their shifts. He needed to call a meeting with them all as soon as possible.

But first, he had some serious thinking to do.

McNiel had been surprised when he'd been chosen for this strange mission to Cameroon. He was less than a year from retirement, and he had suspected the director would stick him behind a desk for his last few months as a federal officer. But that hadn't happened. And the tone of the director's voice, as well as his facial expressions and body language, smelled of someone higher up in the food chain pressuring the man into not only sending men to Cameroon but taking charge of the Secret Service's role in this mess. He would be subordinate only to the big man who called himself Matt Cooper.

A phony moniker if he'd ever heard one.

But the big man had a way about him, McNiel thought, as he crossed his legs on the couch, a way that instilled confidence in the other men on this mission as well as in McNiel himself. Cooper not only looked tougher than any Ultimate Fighting Champion the Secret Service agent had ever seen, he moved with the grace of a cat. A lion or tiger, that was—hardly a house pet. The fact was he reminded McNiel a little bit of Johnny Cash when the "Man in Black" had been in his prime. He just flat had that look about him that said, "Mess with me at your own risk."

Over the years, McNiel had learned a lot about himself. And one of those things was that he resented taking orders from stupid bureaucrats who spent their careers behind a desk and never entered into the action on the street. McNiel had worked the streets all right, both with the Secret Service's Protection Unit and the Counterfeiting Division. In his years he had been a bodyguard for seven different Presidents, various presidential candidates, and all of their families. He had also served as a countersniper and spotter, hiding atop tall buildings and searching the windows and roofs of other tall buildings with a rifle scope or binoculars during presidential convoys.

McNiel had been a kid when John F. Kennedy was assassinated, and he was pretty sure that's what had made him begin to lean toward law enforcement in general, and the Secret Service in particular, as a career.

But why had he been sent here, to Cameroon, for what was undoubtedly an international powder keg just begging to explode? McNiel didn't know. It was promising to be an extremely physical assignment, and he had just barely passed his last yearly physical. He was beginning to have some blockage in the arteries near his heart, and he'd been offered medical retirement on the spot.

But since he had no idea what he'd do in retirement, and it being a borderline case which left it up to him to decide, he had turned it down.

McNiel smiled slightly as he reached into his pocket for a pack of cigarettes. When he pulled them out, he stared at the still-sealed package, then tucked them away again. The smile widened as he thought of what complex people he and his fellow human beings were. As long as he had the cigarettes with him, he knew he could smoke one, or more, if he just *had* to. Which, somehow, kept him from having to. It took the edge off of his addiction, and had worked that way for the last eight months, since he'd quit smoking.

Finally lifting the telephone from the table next to the couch, McNiel tapped in the number for suite 305. A moment later, Tim Robertson—the youngest member of the Secret Service team—picked up the receiver in his room and said, "Yeah, Boss?"

McNiel frowned. Cameroon's telephonic technology was about as far from Caller ID as NASA was from landing a manned mission on the sun. "How'd you know it was me?" McNiel asked.

"High-tech stuff," Robertson said in a jovial tone, and McNiel could almost see the young man's tongue in his cheek. "That, and the fact that Cooper and Lareby are out and you're the only other person who knows what room we're in." He paused, then said, "I guess it could still have been one of the other guys. Call it a lucky guess."

"Well," McNiel said, "I'm so impressed I'll reward you with an assignment. Round up everybody and bring them down here. We need to meet before we hook up with Colonel Essam, his men and the presidential candidates. And keep in mind that this is going to be one booger of a job. We not only have to deal with a colonel who's royally pissed off at our presence, we've also got to protect two homicidal, obnoxious presidential candidates. And we've got to keep them and their men from killing each other at the same time."

"Piece of cake," Robertson said.

"Son," McNiel told him, "if you live long enough, you're going to find out that there's no such thing as a 'piece of cake' in this outfit."

"Yes sir," Robertson said in a more respectful tone of voice.

"And quit calling me sir, dammit," McNiel said. "I've told you before. This isn't the Army, and I feel old enough without you constantly reminding me."

"Yes s—" Robertson stumbled. "I mean, okay, Dennis."

"I want to see everybody in five minutes. Starting now." McNiel glanced at his watch, then sat back against the couch again. "We've got to set up two separate meetings. One with the CPU and their presidential candidate, and another with the KNDP and their man."

"We'll be doing pretty much the same with both factions," Robertson said. "You don't want to just combine the two?"

McNiel suppressed an urge to scream into the young agent's ear. "Did you hear anything I just said about these guys killing each other, Tim?" he said in a controlled voice. "Did you even *look* at the files during the flight over? This isn't like a joint meeting of the House and Senate. Meeting the two groups together would be like dropping a mongoose into a cage with a viper. Or inviting the Hell's Angels and the Outlaws to the same backyard barbeque. They'd shoot each other dead before a single word got said."

"Yes, sir," Robertson said. "I'm sorry, sir. I wasn't thinking."

McNiel finally allowed himself to yell, "And quit calling

me sir!" Then, without further ado, he slammed the receiver back into its cradle.

The Secret Service team leader stared at the phone for a moment, his mind still on Robertson. He was tough on the kid, but that was only because Robertson showed tremendous promise as an agent. The young man had been a rodeo cowboy from New Mexico before injuries forced him to choose another career. The Secret Service had been that choice, but his injuries meant that he had barely squeaked by the agency's preemployment physical.

Not that you'd ever know it from working with him. Robertson was still young and fast, and a deadly shot with a pistol, rifle or shotgun. And the kid could sprint like a cheetah or jog for hours at a speed befitting a marathon winner. Which was just fine with McNiel, who knew, as retirement neared, that he had lost a great deal of the strength and endurance he had once had himself.

All of which made the Secret Service man think of the old featherweight boxing champion, Willie Peps who had once stated, "The first thing to go are your legs. Then your reflexes. Then your friends." The quotation brought a smile to McNiel's face. "Old Willie" had nailed things right on the head. All of his friends were either in the Secret Service or other branches of law enforcement. And when he finally "pulled the pin" as cops called it, he'd be left to some kind of worthless pastime like fly-fishing or golf.

By this point some of the other agents had already begun drifting in through the open doors between the rooms and finding seats. The first to enter the suite were the two men who would make up Team A. Dwight Day was in his midthirties, and he had made a name for himself by stopping a kidnapping attempt on the vice-president's daughter by a group of Middle Eastern terrorists. He'd taken a round in the leg in the process, and the knee he limped in on now was made of steel.

Day was followed by Phillip Fourfeathers, a Kiowa-Caddo Indian from Oklahoma who looked almost as much like a giant redwood tree as he did a man. Fourfeathers's forearms were as big as McNiel's biceps and triceps, and his calves should have been called *cows*.

Fourfeathers was a damn good man to have around in a fight, McNiel knew, whether it be with weapons or bare-handed.

Jason Maynard came next, all decked out in one of the two-thousand-dollar tailored suits for which he was known. Maynard came from a family with money, but that had not softened him in the least. McNiel knew he was also a good man, in spite of his slightly overblown ego and vanity.

Layton Williams followed closely behind Maynard. He was sandy-haired and always looked like his face had been sunburned. Williams and Maynard would make up Team B.

Finally, Morris Deerfield and Tom McLaughlin entered the room. Team C looked ready and willing to take on the action that was sure to come.

Finally, Tim Robertson entered the suite. Due to his age and lack of experience, McNiel had decided to partner Robertson with himself. That way he could moderate the youngster's enthusiasm with experience and common sense. Together, they would be Team D.

When all of the men were finally seated, McNiel stood up and walked to the center of the room. "I'm going to get straight into business," he said. "There's a good deal of danger involved in this undertaking. That was explained to you back in D.C., and you were all given a chance to say no to this assignment. None of you did. But I'm going to give you one last chance." He turned a full circle, letting his eyes fall on each man as he went. "Does anybody want out?"

All of the heads in the room shook back and forth silently.

"Good," McNiel said. He went on to explain that Teams A and B would be in charge of the Kamerun National Democratic Party, and C and D would be assigned to the Cameroon People's Union.

He was about to launch further into the briefing when the sharp crack of a rifle sounded from somewhere outside the window.

For a brief moment, McNiel and the other Secret Service agents sat where they were, quizzical looks on their face.

But that didn't last long.

All of the men inside the living room of suite 307 hit the carpet as soon as they noticed that Robertson was already lying there, bleeding from a head wound.

THE FIRST THING Bolan noted when he kicked the steel door open was the strong fragrance of coffee that hung in the air. It meant that the warehouse had once been, and maybe still was, a storage site for coffee beans—one of Cameroon's primary industries.

But that didn't mean much to Bolan at the moment. He was far more concerned with the fact that rifle rounds were sailing over his head.

Knowing that surprised, inexperienced and frightened men tended to shoot high, the soldier had dived through the opening, hitting the concrete floor even before the door had completely swung back on its hinges. With the big .44 Magnum pistol in his fist, he rolled once to his right to get out of the way of Lareby, who he knew would be following him through the entryway.

Two rifle rounds that sounded as if they'd come from AK-47s hit the concrete where Bolan had been only a second before. He hoped they had not found Lareby as they ricocheted, and concluded that they hadn't when he heard no sound of distress behind him.

As two more rifle rounds—sounding more like 5.56 mm bullets—whizzed over his head, the soldier evaluated the interior of the warehouse. To his right, stored in three huge troughs, were dark brown coffee beans. To his left were three more, similarly filled. The center of the room, where he currently rested on his belly, consisted of nothing more than a long narrow hallway that Bolan assumed led to the front entrance, out of view, around a corner.

Still on his belly, the Executioner ran the Desert Eagle dry of the armor-piercing rounds he had used on the door, taking out two men pointing AK-47s his way. Glancing up as he shoved his last full magazine of RBCD fragmentation rounds into the butt of the Desert Eagle, he saw that the second story of the large building had been floored with plywood.

What was up there was anybody's guess.

But as he let the Desert Eagle's slide fly forward, chambering the first fully fragmenting round, he saw that there were four more men in the narrow passage, behind those he'd just shot. One appeared to be holding an American-made AR-15/M-16, while the other three fumbled in their waistbands or hip holsters for a variety of pistols.

Using the time-honored rule of taking out the most dangerous threat first, the Executioner squeezed two rounds from the Desert Eagle. The first caught the man with the M-16 in the chest, blowing him backward into the middle of the other three. As he collapsed, he knocked one of the other men over the side of the bin and into the coffee beans.

Seeing this gave the remaining two Menye sympathizers an idea, and they both attempted to dive into separate bins.

The Executioner stopped one of the men with a single .44 Magnum round, but the other managed to vault into the coffee beans and dig his way in, out of sight, before Bolan could swing the Desert Eagle that way.

By this point, Lareby had joined in the battle. On his feet, he stayed out of sight of the men in the hallways, moving quickly to the corner of the entryway that led to the narrow walkway. From his peripheral vision, Bolan watched him drop to a kneeling position. The CIA field agent twisted his face and gun hand slightly around the coffee bin. His .380 Walther PPK popped twice before he pulled his head back away from the foray.

Both rounds missed.

Suddenly, the warehouse became silent as the roar from the big .44, the AK-47s and the .380 pistol died down. Bolan rose quietly to his feet, holstering the near-empty Desert Eagle and drawing the Beretta from his shoulder holster. He was certain that none of the men had hidden in the two troughs closest to him. But four other bins of coffee beans stood behind the first—two on each side of the hallway— and it had been impossible to determine exactly which ones contained the still-living Menye supporters who had vaulted the sides.

With the Beretta still pointed forward, Bolan moved toward Lareby to whisper into the man's ear. "There's at least two more gunners," he said. "Likely more. And I don't know what we're going to face on the second floor." His eyes moved to a rickety wooden staircase. At the top was a closed door.

"Then we've got to get the two hiding in the coffee beans and check the front of the warehouse," Lareby whispered back.

The soldier continued to keep his voice down. "Exactly what I was about to say." His eyes moved up and down the narrow hallway again. "And we need to pick up some hardware as we go." He glanced quickly at the chronograph on his wrist.

By this point, Charlie Mott would be a few hours out of Cameroon with the second jet, more ammo, weapons and other gear. But for the moment, they would have to make do with what they could scavenge.

Bolan led the way down the narrow hall, the Beretta aimed in front of him, ready for Menye's men who had burrowed under the beans into hiding.

They could pop up at any moment and open fire.

The first two bodies on the floor that they came to were the ones the Executioner had shot. With one eye on the bins to his left, Bolan leaned down, scooped up one of the AK-47s, checked the chamber to ensure it held a round, then popped the magazine out of the well and looked at it.

The Beretta remained in his left hand as he determined that the magazine had no round indicators on the side, and was not of the transparent type that told the shooter exactly how much firepower was left. But it felt light in the Executioner's hand so, cradling the stock under his arm, he stuck it in the back pocket of his slacks and pulled two more fully loaded box mags from the body on the floor. One went into the weapon. The other found a home in his other back pocket.

Lareby had started toward the M-16 on the floor nearby. Bolan stopped him. "Grab another AK," he said in a low voice. "My guess is that we'll come across more 7.62 mm ammo than we will 5.65s."

Lareby nodded. "But the M-16's more accurate," the CIA man said. "And they've both got slings. I'll just take them both."

Suddenly two of Menye's men rose from under the coffee beans at almost the same time. One held a West German G11 rifle, a weapon that shot a caseless round from a rotating cylinder that aligned the projectile with the breech, then fired. Where he had come across such a rare and curious rifle, Bolan couldn't say.

And he would never find out.

Tapping the trigger of the Beretta once in 3-round-burst mode, Bolan practically beheaded the man holding the exotic weapon with all three rounds tearing into his face. Split and splintered beans flew through the air like harmless shrapnel, and the odor of coffee grew even stronger in the air. The guard was still covered in dark brown beans up to his knees as he fell backward.

In his peripheral vision, Bolan saw Lareby raising his M-16 toward the man who had emerged from the coffee beans in the container next to him. He fired another trio of rounds from the Beretta into that bin.

This 3-round burst hit the X ring in the man's chest. Then the full-metal-jacketed rounds penetrated out of the man's back to "brew" more odiferous coffee inside the storage bin.

The Executioner led the way down the hall, the odor of coffee beans almost overpowering, and mixed with the iron-like smell of fresh blood. Every few feet he stopped and, with his left hand held up behind him, indicated that Lareby should do the same. His eyebrows lowered toward his nose in concentration as he listened. But he heard nothing in front of him, and only Lareby's quiet breathing to his rear.

When he reached the end of the hall, he could see that the last coffee bin on his left used the front of the building as one of its sides. The only foot path available was to the right— toward what Bolan guessed would be another set of rickety wooden steps leading upward. Sneaking an eye around the corner, he saw the stairs.

But no one was on them.

Finally, he holstered the Beretta. The men upstairs could

not possibly have been deaf to the earlier gunfire. And Bolan had made use of the sound-suppressed Beretta only to keep them from pinpointing his exact position as he made his way down the hall. But the time for stealth was once again over.

The Executioner reached beneath the carriage of the AK-47 and flipped the selector to full-auto. Then he stepped around the corner and started toward the stairs.

7

It made no difference how lightly, or slowly, he placed his feet on the floor.

The rotting wood beneath Bolan's hiking boots screamed out his presence with every step. And behind him, he could hear similar creaks as Lareby followed him toward the closed door at the top of the stairs.

Most men—be they soldiers, police officers or other warriors—would have turned back and radioed for backup. But Bolan had no such option.

He and Lareby were both the head and the shaft of the spear.

Finally reaching the step just outside the door, Bolan leaned hard against the wall just to the side of the doorknob. The men inside the second story of the warehouse, who he suspected were protecting former president Menye, didn't know who he was, but they knew he had come and that he was *not* a friend.

Bolan could visualize the barrels of pistols and rifles aimed at the door, just waiting. They would open fire as soon as he opened the door. If it was locked, they would hear him trying to twist the ancient brass doorknob, and the quiet hiss of his Beretta or the roars of the AK-47 when he blew open the lock.

They wouldn't even wait for him to open the door. They'd blast lead through the termite-ridden wood until they were certain he was dead.

Bolan paused, thinking.

Sometimes the best action was no action at all.

And this was one of those times.

Turning to Lareby, the soldier held a finger to his lips for silence, then motioned the CIA man to lean as far to the side of the door as he could. Lareby nodded and followed his partner's silent instructions.

Bolan twisted to his side, making himself even less of a target, and pressed his shoulder even harder against the wall. An inch or so of his chest still stuck out over the door, but there was nothing he could do about that. His only consolation was that if a blind round from the other side *did* find him, it would be a mere flesh wound, which would pass in and out of his body at a shallow angle.

Taking a deep breath, Bolan pressed his ear against the wall. He could hear nothing inside.

But he knew what lay in wait.

Finally reaching out, Bolan grasped the doorknob, rattled it back and forth, then jerked his hand back a split second before a multitude of explosions sounded from the other side, and huge bullet holes appeared in the door only inches from his face.

Almost miraculously, none of the rounds found his chest, but he could feel the heat of the lead as several bullets ripped through his shirt and further tore his sports coat.

Still, the Executioner didn't move.

Breathing shallowly, Bolan and Lareby waited. The gunfire died down for a second, then a few final shots blasted through the rotted wood door. A moment later, the soldier heard quiet steps grow louder as at least one of the men walked toward the staircase to double-check their handiwork.

Bolan heard the same sound he had made when he'd twisted the doorknob earlier, then the door slowly began to open.

The second the Executioner saw the eye peeking through the opening, he angled the AK-47 upward and pulled the trigger. Three rounds of 7.62 mm ammunition spit from the Russian assault rifle and practically tore the head off of a black man with gray hair at the temples. Taking another step upward, Bolan swung the door the rest of the way open and pushed the dead-on-its-feet corpse back and out of the way.

Behind him, the Executioner heard Lareby step up to the position he had just vacated as he dived into the second story of the warehouse.

Flashes of shapes and colors met Bolan's eyes as he curled into a shoulder roll beneath return fire from the Menye supporters. Those shapes and colors told him he had entered an elaborately remodeled living-room-like area of the warehouse, and further persuaded him that this was, indeed, a hideout for the ex-president.

But there was no time, or need, for the Executioner to further evaluate interior decoration. Rolling up onto both knees, he pulled the trigger of the AK-47 and sent a steady stream of fire from the barrel. Beginning on the far left side of the room, he emptied the entire magazine as he gradually swung the weapon to the right, destroying everything in its path. Armed men fell, couches and chairs ripped open, and statuettes and other decorations shattered as Bolan continued to hold the trigger back.

Return fire came, whizzing past his ears so close that it sounded as if he'd stuck his head into a hive of angry wasps.

Rolling again, the Executioner changed both magazines and his position to keep the gunmen from zeroing in on him. It was not a game of staying "a second ahead" of the enemy. It was a game of milliseconds.

The Kalashnikov-designed rifle replenished, Bolan held the trigger back once more. He could tell that Lareby had entered the room from the gunfire that exploded right behind him, and he saw two men he had not yet aimed at fall. The Executioner nodded to himself. Lareby had not yet been tested in full out-and-out battle, but he was proving to be a true soldier as he backed up the Executioner.

Bolan rose to his feet, still firing, as four remaining men ducked through a doorway and out of sight. For a moment, the roar of battle died down.

The soldier took advantage of the short interim to evaluate the scene. Dead men surrounded him. Dressed in everything from traditional African robes to blue jeans and sweatshirts, blazers and ties, they lay awkwardly where they had fallen, their limbs twisted into a parade of grotesque positions.

But none of them looked like the pictures of President Menye that the Executioner had seen.

The man-on-the-run had evidently retreated with the remaining guards from this living-room-like area. If he'd been in this part of the warehouse at all.

Slowly, quietly, Bolan moved across the carpet toward the door through which the remaining quartet of men had disappeared. When he reached it, he took up a position to the right side, much like he'd done earlier on the stairs. But the current situation was far different. Earlier the enemy had focused on the door to the stairs, and this time they would be aware of the "trick" Bolan had utilized, and might open up to shoot through the thin walls of the remodeled warehouse at any moment.

This time, it was the Executioner who would have to make the first move.

Quickly flipping the rifle, Bolan squeezed the pistol grip with his left hand and let his left index finger find the trigger. Silently, he dropped to his knees again, knowing that each second that went by meant another second during which one or more of Menye's men might think about shooting through the wall. Then, without further ado, Bolan leaned out around the doorway and opened fire.

Sweeping the rifle from left to right again, the Executioner sent a half-dozen rounds into an empty kitchen. Pots and pans danced off the countertops, and dishes exploded into pieces in the rack of the open-door dishwasher. The Executioner let up on the trigger as soon as he saw that the enemy had retreated farther into the warehouse-apartment, and the kitchen was empty.

Bolan rose to his feet and glanced quickly behind him.

Lareby stood there, his own AK-47 aimed down at the ground at a forty-five-degree angle.

Bolan held out his fist and curled back a thumb.

Lareby read the signal, then followed the soldier into the kitchen.

With the assault rifle leading the way, Bolan walked quietly across the tile floor. It had recently been mopped, and the odor of pungent cleanser mixed with the more permanent smell of coffee beans that permeated the entire warehouse. The soldier noted that the tile, countertops, refrigerator and other appliances all looked used. His guess was that Menye had set up this safehouse long in advance of his quick departure from office. Maybe he had known the day would eventually come when he'd have to go into hiding. Or perhaps he had created this secluded apartment as a "love nest" for secret rendezvous. Maybe both.

Not that it mattered much any longer. Regardless of its

original role, it had become a convenient place for Menye to hide out while keeping tabs on the action taking place in Cameroon.

The Executioner crept slowly across the tiles, stepping over and around the broken pieces of ceramic and glass he had created. Another door on the other side of the kitchen led yet deeper into the warehouse-apartment, and it had to be through this opening that Menye's men had retreated. When he came to the open doorway, Bolan used the same strategy that had worked for him twice already—he leaned hard against the wall to the right of the door.

But he knew that the men he sought had seen this tactic when he'd first entered the apartment. There was a good chance at least one of them had not pulled his head back out of sight until after the Executioner did the same thing before opening fire in the kitchen. So he varied the technique this time by staying on his feet and shooting from full height.

Which was good. Because when he swung his arms and shoulders around the corner, dozens of automatic rounds blew by below him—where his head and chest would have been had he been kneeling. As it was, he could feel the heat as the lead streaked past.

As he returned fire, the Executioner caught a glimpse of a bedroom. Two dressers, a small desk, and a large king-size bed. Pulling the trigger, he got a man wearing a worn and crumpled Cincinnati Reds baseball cap squarely between the eyes. One round hit the bridge of his nose, exploding his face like a watermelon dropped from a ten-story building. A second 7.62 mm from the AK-47 disappeared somewhere into the blood and other gore that remained atop his neck.

Bolan swung his rifle slightly to the left—to the other side of the doorway where only the barrel of a rifle, half a face and a bright yellow shirt could be seen. Raising his aim slightly, he fired his rifle for a quick kill.

Another head exploded in the doorway.

Suddenly, the passageway was clear again, and silence fell over the apartment.

Bolan leaned back, taking cover once again against the wall next to the door leading out of the kitchen. A quick glance behind him showed that Lareby still followed. So far, the man had not been in a position to fire even one shot, and the look on the CIA agent's face told Bolan that he was chomping at the bit to get in on the action.

Bolan took a deep breath as he updated his strategy. He didn't know how many more men were waiting in the remainder of the makeshift dwelling. But it appeared that the reconstruction of the second floor of the warehouse circled all the way around the building.

So roughly half of it remained to be cleared.

Menye, the Executioner suspected, would have taken shelter in the very farthest recesses of the apartment. Perhaps another bedroom or bathroom. At this point, it was impossible to know.

Inching his face back around the doorway, Bolan saw only the corpses of the two men he had just shot. So, with his eyes wide open and his senses on high, he stepped into the bedroom and moved toward yet another door.

He was halfway across the room when a hand holding an old and blue-worn Colt Python snaked out from under the bed, pointed upward. The Executioner had already returned his AK-47 to his right hand, and, twisting his arm toward the deadly .357 Magnum pistol, he fired.

An anguished yelp was vaguely audible over the roar of the three 7.62 mm rounds that blew from the Kalashnikov's barrel, practically severing the hand holding the wheel gun. As the revolver fell from what little remained of that hand, the Executioner heard more AK-47 fire from behind him.

In his peripheral vision, Bolan saw Lareby holding the

trigger back on his own Soviet assault rifle. The CIA man was making the quilt jump, and mattress stuffing flew into the air as his rounds penetrated the bedding and made the visible wrist go limp.

As the explosions died down, only the singing of the steel coils in the box springs could be heard as they vibrated within the bed.

The Executioner pulled the fresh magazine from his back pocket, changed it out with the partially spent box in the AK-47, hooked the top into the notch at the front of the action, then twisted it home. The partial load took up new residence in his slacks. Turning a full 360 degrees, he made sure there were no more of Menye's men hiding in this bedroom to ambush him. The only other possible place of concealment was behind what appeared to be a closet door. It was closed tightly.

Bolan looked into Lareby's eyes, then nodded toward the door.

The CIA man understood. Moving softly across the bedroom carpet, Lareby kept his rifle aimed at the next doorway, leading out of the bedroom. When he reached the closet, he stepped to the side, then reached out with his left hand and grasped the doorknob. Looking back to the Executioner, he waited until Bolan had raised his own rifle and nodded. Then he twisted to knob and pulled the door open, covering himself.

One of Menye's guards had been standing there, patiently awaiting this opportunity with an Uzi submachine gun gripped in both fists. He was partially hidden by the hung clothing his body had misplaced inside the small area. But there was plenty for Bolan to see as he fired the first few rounds from the new AK-47 magazine, and the man's body jerked back and forth, up and down. A split second later,

Lareby joined in the firefight, shooting through the gap just between the upper and middle hinges of the door.

The room was cleared once more as the man's lifeless form fell forward onto the carpet.

Taking the lead yet again, the soldier moved to the next door. The apartment seemed to circle the top floor of what had once undoubtedly housed more coffee bean bins. The odor of coffee still hung in the air—almost as strong as on the bottom floor. It was a smell that would stay with the building—regardless of how many reconstructions it went through—until the warehouse was completely torn down and the lumber scrapped.

Bolan took up a position on the left side of the door this time. Pulling a tiny mirror from his shirt pocket, he positioned it so he could see the room without exposing any of his body except his thumb and index finger. He and Lareby had worked their way around to the opposite side of the building from where they'd started, and rather than another bedroom as Bolan had guessed, this final large room appeared to be a conference area. A long wooden table, with a freshly polished top and wheeled chairs circling it, took up most of the room. What space was still available, however, was filled with the remainder of Menye's personal guards.

The ex-president didn't believe in traveling light, Bolan realized. There were at least ten men still breathing, and they stood shoulder to shoulder at the other end of the room, waiting as if they were about to stubbornly defend the Alamo or the rocky gates of Thermopylae.

Partially visible behind the men, Bolan could see two more doors. One, he suspected, led to another set of rickety stairs. The other could not possibly hide anything but a small room—they were running out of building. He had not encountered any bathroom facilities so far, so his bet was that a toilet, sink and shower were behind that door.

The Executioner pulled the mirror back, thankful that none of the men inside the conference room had spotted it. Lareby, as usual, was right behind him and all Bolan had to do was look over his shoulder and whisper, "About ten. I'm going in low, and I'll start at the left. You go high, and work from the right."

"Meet you in the middle," the CIA field op whispered back.

"On three." Bolan held up his left index finger, then his middle finger and finally added his ring finger before diving through the opening onto his belly.

Shooting from the prone position, the Executioner had fired half a magazine of 7.62 mm rounds before the men inside the room could even respond to what was happening. The four guards on the left all jerked like stringed marionettes being manipulated by an insane puppet master. Two of them fell forward onto the table into the huge pool of blood, bone fragments and intestinal matter that had preceded them, while the other two were blown backward against the front wall of the warehouse.

As if from somewhere far in the distance, the Executioner heard the sound of Lareby's AK as the CIA man mowed down the men on the right. Swinging his own assault rifle toward the middle of the pack, Bolan pulled the trigger again.

And nothing happened.

Without thinking, the Executioner employed what was known as a tap, rack bang drill, striking the end of the magazine with the palm of his hand, pulling the bolt back and letting it fall forward again. Then he squeezed the trigger once more.

The tap—really a forceful smack—went fine.

So did the rack.

But, again, the bang didn't come when he squeezed the trigger.

By this point the remaining guards were reacting to the attack, and several rounds blew past the soldier's head. Letting the malfunctioning rifle fall from his hands, Bolan rolled to his side and drew the Desert Eagle. The giant .44 Magnum semiauto pistol jumped in his hand, sending an RBCD total-fragmentation round squarely into the middle of the shooter's chest and knocking him back against the closed doorway the Executioner had spotted in the mirror.

It was as if a load of C-4 plastic explosives had gone off in the man's heart. As the tiny particles of lead from the softpoint round separated, a huge red, misty cloud appeared in front of the man. He fell back against the door, which opened to reveal a sink.

And yet another hiding bodyguard.

The man was standing sideways in the doorway, and Bolan's next RBCD round hit him in the upper arm. Another, smaller red cloud appeared, and while it nearly tore the man's arm from his shoulder, few of the fragments went on to penetrate his chest. What they did do, however, was spin the man to face him, and another squeeze of the trigger opened a major cavity in the guard's head.

Lareby had continued firing, and when Bolan turned his attention back to the remaining men, he saw that only two remained standing. Another .44 Magnum round downed the man closer to the left. And Lareby's well-functioning AK-47 dropped the last.

For what was about the fourth time in the long-ranging gunfight on the second floor of the warehouse, silence fell over the apartment.

On the floor, Bolan's eyes skirted between the legs and wheels of the conference chairs, searching for anyone hiding there. He found no one.

Lareby didn't have to be told to check the bathroom. As he eyed the tangled chairs beneath the table, Bolan heard the swish of a shower curtain being pulled back.

But no shots rang out.

Lareby returned to the conference room and shook his head at the soldier as Bolan rose back to his feet.

"Go get Antangana," Bolan said. "We need to know which one of these guys is Menye."

The CIA man nodded, turned toward the final closed door and kept his rifle in the ready position as he twisted the knob.

Bolan stood back and helped him cover the area as the door swung open. But just as he'd guessed, all they saw was the same rotting set of wooden steps leading downward.

Since they had worked their way all around the top of the building, it didn't take long for Lareby to return with Antangana. The man's face said it all. The diplomat was visibly shaken and physically shivering, having heard all of the gunfire inside the building. With each shot, he'd wondered if it would be Bolan and Lareby who would eventually come for him, or if Menye's men would prove victorious and shoot him last.

"I know it's unsettling," Bolan told the man as soon as Lareby had led him into the room, "but we need you to take a good look. It's imperative that we ID Menye."

Antangana nodded, moving slowly from one corpse to another, showing all of the signs of the fatigue produced by chemotherapy. Occasionally, he raised his open hand to his throat in an obvious attempt to keep from vomiting. But each time he viewed a man, he shook his head. Bolan began to get an uneasy feeling.

The Executioner led the way, retracing their steps from the conference room, into the bedroom, then crossing the empty kitchen into the living room where the firefight had first begun.

But Antangana continued to shake his head.

Finally, they had reached the front door. Antangana had seen all of the bodies inside the warehouse and shaken his head each time. Bolan led him down the building's stairs to look at the bodies between, and in, the coffee bins on the ground floor. But by this point the uneasiness had turned to resolve, as he came to terms with one simple, unfortunate fact.

Menye wasn't in the warehouse. Dead or alive.

"I am sorry," Antangana finally said as he looked up into the soldier's eyes. "I recognize many of the men who were bodyguards during the years when Menye was in office. But the ex-president is not here."

8

The fact that they had heard no police sirens since the long gun battle began reinforced what the Executioner had been told about this section of Yaounde.

Violence, including gunfire, was a nightly occurrence. No big deal. At least not a big enough deal for any survival-oriented Cameroonian cop to risk his own life over.

As if reading his mind, Antangana looked up at Bolan and said, "We can take our time searching this place if you like. Even the police do not enter this area of the city before the sun comes up."

"Then let's see what we can find," Bolan said. They had returned to the conference area, and he stepped into the bathroom, dropped to one knee and began going through the pockets of the man who had just recently fallen to his rifle-fire.

The man had worn tight straight-legged jeans. Obviously new and yet-to-be-washed, they were so dark navy blue they looked almost black under the dim overhead light. The pockets were empty, as were those of his shirt.

The dead man lay on his back, and the soldier drew the knife from the sheath at the small of his back. The curved belly of the blade made short work of the laces holding the man's desert-tan combat boots together. Bolan pulled them off the gunner's feet and examined the insides, then removed the socks. No ankle guns or knives, no driver's license or other documents.

Nothing.

Rising to his feet, Bolan saw Lareby and Antangana performing similar searches on the other bodies scattered around the conference room. Working backward, they scoured the remains of the other men who had died in the various rooms on the second floor of the warehouse. But they found nothing more interesting than a pair of theater ticket stubs, several more South African Okapi folding knives, and one tiny .22 Short North American Arms minirevolver.

Bolan lifted the minute firearm. It was so small it could be held with his thumb behind his fingers and completely disappear. Yet it was chambered to hold five rounds of .22 Short bullets.

The soldier was no stranger to NAA's wide range of tiny wheel guns, and had made good use of some of them in the past. But as he looked down at the end of the cylinder, he frowned.

Something about this .22 Short was different.

Pulling out the cylinder pin, Bolan dumped the five .22s into the palm of his hand and immediately snapped to what had caught his trained eye. The lead bullets at the mouth of the cartridge were barely visible—they had been sanded down. Glancing at the end of one of the rimfire cartridges, he saw that this ammunition was actually .22 Long.

The Executioner nodded. Someone—probably the dead man before him—had shortened the lead projectile to make it fit into the .22 Short. That had resulted in a much lighter bullet propelled by more powder at a far faster speed.

Menye's bodyguard was no rookie. He had known his guns and ammo. While it was still no .45 or .44 Magnum, the little wheel gun had suddenly been promoted out of the category that limited it to soft targets such as the eyes, nostrils or throat. While a round or two to the chest still wouldn't take down an assailant as quickly as the Executioner's Desert Eagle or even the Beretta 93-R, it far transcended the ballistics for which it had been designed.

Death might take a little longer, and it might take two or three rounds to bring it about, but it would come.

And dead was dead, no matter what instrument was used to bring it about.

Bolan dropped the tiny handgun into the side pocket of his worn and torn sports coat. If the resupply plane from the U.S. didn't get here soon, he was going to have to discard the garment altogether and do his best to hide his weaponry beneath his shirt.

Which wasn't in much better shape than the jacket.

By the time they'd finished searching the dead men on the second floor, it had become obvious to Bolan that these supposed guards had "sterilized" themselves, an old slang spy term for making sure there was no incriminating evidence, or any other clues on their bodies, to suggest where they'd been, where they were going, or what they were doing.

"Gather up all the rifles, pistols, and extra ammo you can find and dump them on the bedspread," Bolan ordered Lareby and Antangana. "We may need them until the resupply plane gets here."

The two men hurried to comply.

When the various firearms and knives were on the bed, Bolan jerked the corners of the bedspread from the mattress and tied the corners together. Antangana and Lareby each took an end of the makeshift gun case and followed Bolan down the steps to the first floor. They set the weapons down as soon as they'd reached the bottom floor and began searching the bodies that had fallen there.

The soldier wasn't at all shocked when they found nothing of interest on them, either.

What *did* slightly surprise him, however, was the sudden vibration in the front pocket of his ripped and torn slacks. Pulling out his satellite phone, he looked into the caller ID window and saw that Grimaldi was trying to reach him.

"Yeah, Jack?" Bolan said, as he pressed the phone to his ear.

"The planes are almost here," the ace "flyboy" said. "You may want to head toward the airport. They'll have landed by the time you get there."

"Great," the Executioner said, glancing down at a long rip down the side of his slacks. "I'm beginning to look like a scarecrow."

"Well," Grimaldi said, "you never were a candidate as a model for *Gentleman's Quarterly*."

"Point taken," he said. "But Lareby and I are at a point where we're going to draw attention."

A sudden loud creak above him caused Bolan to look up at the ceiling of the warehouse. It looked to be made of plywood, and held a fairly fresh coating of green paint. But it was nailed to the old and rotting wood of the rest of the warehouse, and he had heard almost constant squeaking between gunshots ever since he'd entered the building. But this creak had been louder than the others, and he turned his attention back to the phone.

Bolan changed the subject as the background noise on the other end of the line suddenly caught his attention. "Where are you Jack?" he said. "It doesn't sound like a hospital behind you. Did I just hear a plane engine?"

"You did," the pilot said. "I'd had enough of the hospital. Even the sponge baths. I released myself on my own recognizance."

The soldier knew there was no point in trying to get the

Stony Man pilot back into a hospital bed. "Did you say the 'planes,' *plural,* were about to land?" As he spoke, he watched Lareby and Antangana lift the gun-packed comforter and prepare to leave the warehouse.

"I did," Grimaldi said. "Mott's flying our replacement plane with all the gear. Hal called one of the blacksuits to pilot the third jet, which'll take Charlie back. They've got to pick up Phoenix Force in Uganda on the return, anyway."

Bolan let a hard smile curl his lips. Next to Grimaldi, Charlie Mott was the best pilot he had ever known. And many of the Farm's blacksuits were members of the military, rotated to Stony Man for a tour of duty. Several top pilots were always on-site. Hal Brognola—director of the Sensitive Operations at Stony Man Farm—often used a blacksuit pilot when his top two pilots were already engaged.

"I hope you've warned them about what happened to the last plane," Bolan said into the phone. "And I also hope that the airport's covered better this time."

Grimaldi let out a laugh on the other end. "You ought to see this place," he said. "And I guess you will. Prepare yourself for so many fancy uniforms and gold braids that if they were carrying trombones instead of rifles, you'd think you were at a band festival."

Bolan suppressed a smile. "So the airport's full of fancy-dressed military men," he said. "The problem is that nobody really knows what side they're on." He paused to clear his throat. "We can't be sure where anyone's true loyalties are, with the Cameroons, the Kameruns, or on the independent side who want to establish a democracy."

"And therein lies the rub, as Willie Shakespeare would have said," Grimaldi came back.

Bolan had stepped out of the warehouse and into the alley, followed by Lareby and Antangana. "Okay, Jack," he said as he looked up at the brightly lit night sky. "We'll grab a cab and head your way. In addition to mine and Lareby's equipment, is Charlie bringing more supplies for the Secret Service teams?"

"Affirmative," Grimaldi said.

"Okay," Bolan said. "I'll contact them and have them come in behind Lareby and me at the airport. I don't want all of the American faces standing out there at the same time."

"Good thinking," Stony Man Farm's top pilot said.

Bolan ended the call and tapped in the number to connect with Secret Service Special Agent Dennis McNiel. He had planned to give the man a quick briefing as to what he, Lareby and Antangana had just done in the warehouse. But before he could speak McNiel told him about Robertson and the sniper.

"How bad's the head wound?' Bolan asked. McNiel's tone of voice had betrayed nothing, making Bolan suspect it wasn't fatal.

"He was lucky," McNiel confirmed a second later. "It just grazed his forehead and he never even lost consciousness. I had Fourfeathers and Deerfield drive him to the hospital to get checked out, though." McNiel paused. "I think he may have a concussion. He was acting a little loopy before they left. Said he'd been kicked a lot harder by both broncos and bulls when he was on the rodeo circuit. Then he started laughing, and speculating on how the scar was going to help him with girls in bars after he'd cooked up a better story to tell them about how he got it."

Bolan shook his head. "He's a good kid, Dennis," he said. "I can tell that just by being around him. And rodeo cowboys have to be tough. On the other hand, he needs experience. Law-enforcement experience, and by that I mean *real* experience in the *real* world."

"I'll add a big 10-4 to that one, Cooper," McNiel agreed. "You think he'll be fit for duty?"

"I'm no doctor," McNiel said, "but my guess would be yes."

"Any idea on who the sniper was?" Bolan asked.

"KNDP, CPU, the men Menye took with him when he fled office," McNiel said. "Take your pick. It could have been any of them."

"What did Colonel Essam have to say about all this?" he asked.

"I just got off the phone with him," McNiel replied. "He and his men didn't see anything. They didn't even hear the shot or know about it until I called them."

"They're not just useless, they're a liability in their incompetence," the soldier said.

"Welcome to the wonderful world of politics," McNiel said sarcastically. "According to our director, the President— the *American* President—insisted on having native Cameroonian troops working with us. If things blow up, he doesn't want it to look like the U.S. orchestrated a takeover."

"Well," Bolan said, "Essam's made no secret of the fact that he resents us even being in the country, let alone doing his job for him. Then again, he could be telling the truth. If his men were all in their cars with the windows rolled up, their roving patrol might have been roving on the other side of the block or something.

"This shot that hit Robertson," he went on, "might have just been an isolated incident instead of an attack by the KDNP or CPU. After all, they hit your man instead of one of the candidates. You remember the Shoe Bomber and the Underwear Bomber and that U.S. Army colonel who went nuts at Fort Hood, Texas, awhile back?" He didn't wait for an answer. "Started shooting his fellow soldiers? Just a lone Muslim, not associated with any of the Islamic terrorist groups."

"I remember," McNiel said. "He was torn between the

Koran and the U.S. Army. He was finally stopped by a local female police officer who was wounded herself in the process."

Bolan took a moment to look back on it. The case had been a rarity in America at the time. But such suicide, kamikaze-like attacks had become commonplace all over the Middle East and northern Africa. This sniper attack told him nothing about whether it had come from a sole shooter or a representative of the KDNP, CPU, or some other terrorist organization. Bolan just flat didn't know.

He switched his mind back toward the matter at hand. "Okay, then," he told McNiel. "Go ahead and have Essam set up the meetings with the KNDP and CPU and their respective Secret Service teams."

"Will do," McNiel said.

Finally, the soldier gave the Secret Service SAC the rundown on the gunfight at the warehouse.

"You've had a full day, too," McNiel said in an understatement.

"It's not over yet," Bolan said. "Our supply planes are getting close. It'll be an hour, maybe an hour and a half before we get to the airport. Again, I don't like the idea of all of the Westerners being on display at the same time."

"Understood and agreed upon," McNiel said.

Bolan stuck the phone back into his pocket. Turning toward the other two men, he noted that Lareby's clothing was not quite as ripped, torn or smudged as his own. That was because the gun battle in the warehouse had been almost a linear march through the second floor, and Bolan had paved the way with his kneeling, diving and rolling, which allowed Lareby to serve primarily as backup.

There was no telling what they might run into on the way out of this Yaounde ghetto before they reached an area of the city where cabdrivers weren't afraid to pick up fares. They'd already been attacked once on their way to the warehouse. And there was no guarantee that they wouldn't run into other gangs of marauding street thugs on their way back.

"The supply plane is almost here," he said. "So let's destroy these weapons rather than lug them around. But hang on to a rifle until we get out of this neighborhood," he told the CIA man.

Lareby nodded. A moment later, he and Antangana had dropped the comforter to the alley floor and were bashing rifle stocks and pistols against the brick wall of the alley. They kept two of the better-looking AK-47s and several extra magazines, rolling them back up in the comforter.

Retracing their steps, Bolan and Lareby held the AK-47s in front of them in the ready position as they strode forward. Antangana stayed between and slightly behind them. If gangs saw them, they stayed in hiding to wait on easier-looking prey.

When they reached the edge of the ghetto and saw ordinary-looking people walking the streets, Bolan stopped at the end of the alley they traveled. Unrolling the comforter in the shadows of the buildings all around him, he yanked the magazines from both AK-47s and broke the rifles by leaning them on the curb between the sidewalk and the street, then stepping on them. A loud snap sounded both times the Soviet-made weapons broke in two. But no one else on the dark streets paid any attention. Bolan left the rifles there in pieces, satisfied that they could never be used again.

Antangana looked the least threatening of the three, so Bolan placed him out front to flag down a cab. Bolan and Lareby stayed in the shadows until one of the taxis finally pulled over. The driver sat where he was, smiling as he let the prime minister open the back door.

The smile fell from his face when Bolan and Lareby got into the back and Antangana took the shotgun seat. The driver looked the two men over, obviously frightened that he was about to be robbed and possibly murdered.

Antangana smiled. "Do not worry, my friend," he told the driver. "We are, as they say in American Western movies, the good guys."

The driver didn't look very convinced.

"Take us to the airport," Bolan said in a pleasant voice.

The driver nodded nervously, threw the vehicle into gear and took off.

The cab reached the airport as the sun began to rise, just in time to see two unmarked jets setting down on the runways.

9

Charlie Mott and Leon Winters, the blacksuit pilot, walked into the terminal shoulder to shoulder. "Looks like *Sergeant Pepper's Lonely Hearts Club Band* around here," Mott said with his tongue firmly in his cheek as he looked around at the odd mixture of fancy dress uniforms filling the building. "Somebody having a parade?"

Bolan shook hands with both men as he took in the scene himself. It did, indeed, seem as if everyone in the Cameroonian military who had not been officially called to duty to protect the airport had donned their formal attire—complete with ribbons and medals—and shown up anyway.

"I think they just want to make sure that what happened to our airplane doesn't happen to these two," Lareby said. He offered his hand to both men, and Bolan made quick introductions.

Moving to a corner near the glass wall that faced the runways, they joined Grimaldi. "Thanks for the new ride," the ace pilot told Mott. "Leon, good to see you again."

Winters nodded and smiled.

"Let's get out there, get changed and restock," Bolan said. "We've been operating with second-rate, scavenged equipment and wearing rags long enough." As he led the way to the door, he caught a glimpse of Antangana on the other side of the crowded terminal room. The man looked exhausted, as if he might fall to the floor at any moment. The big American had instructed the prime minister to steer clear of them while they were at the airport. Although his face was not as recognizable as that of the former president, or several other high-ranking leaders of this nation in chaos, Bolan didn't want him being seen with them.

Who knew how many of the men wearing Cameroonian battle or formal dress were actually still loyal to Menye? Or how many were secretly aligned with the KDNP or CPU? Bolan wasn't interested in being seen with his primary informant, guide and interpreter unless it became absolutely necessary.

The Americans shook hands once more before Mott and Winters broke off and headed toward the plane that would pick up Phoenix Force—one of the counterterrorist teams that worked out of Stony Man Farm—and then return to the U.S. Bolan let Grimaldi lead the way up the steps and into the new jet that they'd be working from going forward.

As Grimaldi dropped behind the controls, Bolan ducked under the door to the cabin and strode purposefully toward the rear of the plane. Like the jet that had brought the team to Cameroon in the first place, the passenger area had been completely redesigned. Where the seats had once been, reclining chairs now sat in a circle around the room. Bolted securely to the floor and even supplied with seat belts, they had been installed in order to allow Bolan or whoever was using the revamped aircraft to catch up on sleep whenever they were in the air.

But circling the chairs on the outside were several rows of lockers that were stocked with clothing and every sort of weapon and other piece of battle equipment imaginable.

The soldier began walking along the lockers, opening

doors and shedding his shredded sports coat, slacks and shirt
as he went. There was a multitude of clothing in various sizes
from which to choose, and he thought carefully about each
item before picking them out. As Grimaldi had said, he was
no *GQ* model, but he knew that certain types of clothing sent
messages. And since there was absolutely no way a white
man—especially one as big as he was—was going to pass
for a native Cameroonian, the next best thing was to give off
the impression that he and Lareby were tourists.

Out of the corner of his eye, the Executioner saw Lareby
looking in the lockers, too. The safari-style vest he had worn
had escaped the damage Bolan's sports coat had suffered.
The CIA man slid it off his shoulders, pulled a plain white
T-shirt from one of the lockers, shrugged into it and put the
light green vest back on.

The next item the Executioner discarded was his slacks.
They were torn and soiled, and looked as dirty as if he'd just
come off a shift as an oil field roughneck. Stepping into the
legs of a pair of faded Levi's boot cut jeans, he zipped them
up before threading a thick brown leather belt through the
loops.

In the next locker down Bolan found a red 2X T-shirt
which read Pamplona, España on the top of the chest. It
had an embroidered picture of a bull chasing a running
man dressed in a white shirt and white pants, with a red
sash around his waist. Beneath the picture, the words read in
English "I survived."

A small smile slowly stretched across the Executioner's
face. "I survived" might well have been the motto for his
career, and he had survived far more danger than anyone who
had ever caught a horn running with the bulls in Pamplona.
The shirt, however, would give exactly the kind of impression that he wanted to project. By looking as if he'd stopped
in Spain long enough to take part in the legendary festival

before coming on to Cameroon, it suggested to anyone who looked at it that he was a risk taker and would subtly explain his presence in a country most travelers were carefully avoiding.

That was good. It didn't blast to the world *warrior,* but it also accounted for the multiple bullet, blade and other scars on his arms beneath the T-shirt's sleeves. What was bad about the shirt, however, was that it provided little cover for his weapons. The Beretta 93-R had a big frame as 9 mm weapons went, even without the sound suppressor in place. Once that vital piece of equipment was added, it became even larger and longer. The Desert Eagle was simply enormous on its own, and the various extra magazines, as well as the TOPS Loner fixed blade knife, all added to the bulk that would have to be secured around his chest and waist. And a thin T-shirt—no matter what it read on the front—was going to have so many bulky items stretching it out that the Executioner might as well have worn the equipment with no cover garment at all. Alone, the shirt would be as obvious as a rectangular yellow sign that read Weapons on Board!

Looking further, Bolan found a khaki canvas vest cut similarly to the green one Lareby wore. Worn extensively by American journalists and tourists both, it was slightly large in 3X but he knew that tiny oversize would disappear quickly once his equipment was beneath it. And the material was thick and stiff enough that it would not conform to the shape of his guns or other gear.

Donning the Pamplona T-shirt, the Executioner slid back into his shoulder rig and snapped the keeper strap on the holster to his belt. He then adjusted the positioning of the extra 9 mm magazines under his right arm to suit him before anchoring it to the belt on that side. A full-length mirror was mounted on the wall of the jet between two of the lockers, and Bolan made use of it, standing, bending over, reaching above his head and twisting his torso to make sure all of the straps and other components remained concealed.

Remembering the tiny North American Arms .22 Short minirevolver with the homemade high-velocity ammo, he pulled it out of his ruined slacks and dropped it into one of the vest pockets. Satisfied that it presented no signature of its own, Bolan unhooked the leather belt again and threaded the hip holster with the Desert Eagle in it past two loops and into a strong side carry. A double magazine holder—one filled with RBCD total fragmentation rounds like the ones he already had loaded into the big Magnum pistol—the other housing more pointed armor-piercing bullets that would literally shoot through the engine block of a car—snapped onto his belt just in front of where the Beretta's sound suppressor fell. The Loner knife, secured in its holster, returned to the small of his back.

Bolan returned to the mirror, waiting while Lareby checked himself out in a pair of lightweight pants that could be unzipped just above the knees and turned into shorts. Bolan tried hard to spot the man's Walther PPK but couldn't.

"Where's that little mouse gun of yours?" he asked the CIA man in a good-natured tone.

Lareby laughed, then pointed to one of the flapped cargo pockets in his pants. It bulged from the front of his thigh but had no telltale shape. For all anyone seeing it might know, the pocket could have been filled with maps, notebooks and pens, or anything else a vacationer or reporter might carry.

"I found a pocket holster that fit it back there," the CIA agent said, shrugging slightly behind him at several open locker doors. "Couple of extra PPK magazines, too."

"Then you're still going with the .380?" Bolan asked.

"Oh, yeah," Lareby answered with a grin. "It's my favorite

gun." He paused a moment but then added, "Of course I've taken a lesson from you, as well."

Grabbing the unzipped vest in the front with both hands, Lareby spread it like wings. The pants the CIA field agent had chosen were far too light to hold up any full-size pistol without falling down. But Lareby, too, had found a leather belt that passed through the loops around his waist, and Bolan spotted a matching pair of Colt Commander .45s tucked inside the leather.

Both pistols had the hammers back and the ambidextrous thumb safeties on. Cocked and locked was what this method of carry was usually called.

The soldier nodded his approval but remained silent as he bent to the floor to replace the short hiking boots he'd worn earlier with a similar, less torn-up pair. As he did, he watched himself in the mirror. With the two .44 magazines positioned so far to the front, he had been forced to zip his vest to keep them unseen. But now, as he bent, they bulged against the canvas in a most suspicious manner.

Bolan stared at his reflection long after his boots had been tied. Then, slowly, he began unzipping the vest. To open it all the way would again expose the extra mags. But each inch he lowered it took another bite out of the tension against the carrier.

By the time he had pulled the zipper roughly three-quarters of the way down, the bulge had all but disappeared. And when he stood up, it was gone altogether. Bolan turned back to Lareby.

The man had slid his feet back into his own brown hiking boots and was stuffing the remaining cargo pockets of his pants with loaded .45 magazines. Bunched together as they were, they showed no discernable shape any more than the pocket-holstered PPK, which had become the CIA man's backup piece.

Walking to the end of the lockers, Bolan opened the final three. From the first, he pulled an M-16 A-2 and a half-dozen magazines loaded with 5.56 mm hollowpoint rounds. Laying the rifle across one of the reclining chairs behind him, he pulled out a Heckler & Koch MP-5 submachine gun and set it next to the M-16. From the last locker, he produced a custom-made sniper rifle he had designed himself with the help of John "Cowboy" Kissinger, the chief armorer of Stony Man Farm. Composed of a wooden McMillan stock fitted to a target-contoured Shilen bull barrel, it was chambered for .243-caliber rifle rounds. The Leupold VARI-X scope could easily zero in at a thousand yards or farther, and working in conjunction with the range finder and Bolan's skill, could be adjusted for windage and elevation and keep 5-round groups—the maximum number of rounds the sniper rifle would hold with one chambered—inside an inch.

Bolan had sighted in several on the Stony Man Farm firing range before boarding the plane for Cameroon. The custom-made rifle was what was sometimes referred to as a nail driver and did exactly what it had been built to do.

The Executioner started to close the locker door, but just then the dull black finish of a 12-gauge shotgun caught his eye and he pulled it out, too. Bolan snapped the 25-round drum in place and added several 10-round mags to the growing pile of weapons on the chair. Then he turned and looked down at them.

He frowned. There were lockers aboard the plane that he knew were packed with black Kevlar weapons bags specifically made to store and carry all of his firearms. But, again, he needed to transport his firepower in a manner that didn't draw attention. Bolan turned back toward Lareby, then moved past the CIA man to a locker behind him. Inside the OD-green storage area, he found several colorful but nondescript touristy suitcases with wheels at the bottom and collapsible handles on the top. One was long enough to conceal the 12-gauge shotgun and the sniper rifle. And he packed the areas around the two long guns with the extra magazines, boxes of ammo and three blacksuits—one for him, another for Lareby, and one for Antangana—on the off-chance that the bureaucrat would need to go black.

Bolan zipped the zippers, then took a step back, satisfied that his luggage appeared more likely to carry snorkels and swimsuits than guns and ammunition. He was about to close the locker doors when he spotted a tiny flash of stainless steel on a shelf at the top of the locker. He knew what it was and reached up, pulling it out. What he found in his hand appeared to be a normal, everyday, soft-sided eyeglass holder with a short shirt pocket clip on one side. But when he squeezed the sides slightly to open the top, he saw the wooden butt of a tiny pistol inside.

Grasping the wood with both hands, Bolan pulled out the North American Arms Earl. The Earl was the latest innovation of the top-quality minirevolvers that NAA manufactured. He already had the .22 Short that he'd taken from one of the bodies at Menye's warehouse hideout, but over his long career the Executioner had learned that you never had too many weapons until they adversely affected your movement and maneuverability. The Earl had the general shape of an old single-action Remington, and an under-the-barrel release that looked like the loading pins of the early black powder Colts and Remingtons. The pin protected the catch that held the cylinder in place.

But much like the sniper rifle, Kissinger had gone to work on the minirevolver and improved it for Bolan's specific needs. He had shortened the stock 4-inch barrel to 3 inches to make the .22 Magnum weapon fit into the seemingly harmless eyeglass case.

His khaki vest had a special pocket for sunglasses and

cases, so the Executioner clipped the case housing the Earl into that pocket. Then, pulling the .22 Short minirevolver out of his vest, he caught Lareby's eye and said, "Here. A good-luck piece," and tossed the customized .22 Short gun to the CIA agent.

Lareby didn't know what he had caught until he looked down at it. But when he did, the sight brought a wide smile to his face. "You can never be too rich, too skinny, or have too many backups," he finally said.

Bolan nodded. "Or go after your enemies too quickly," he said, then added, "Let's go find out where Menye really is, and what he's up to."

"Whatever it is, it isn't good," Lareby said.

"No," the soldier agreed. "It isn't. And that's why we're going to find him and either bring him in for the International Criminal Court or kill him and all the rest of his men."

10

Robert Menye was as angry as he'd ever been in his life.

At least a third of his bodyguards, men who had sworn allegiance to him when he left office, had been wiped out.

Right in front of his very eyes. And by only two men.

Menye had been forced to wait patiently as the big American in the torn blue blazer and his partner in the safari vest went room to room, annihilating the men in the upstairs apartment of the warehouse. The plywood ceiling had been fortified with both Kevlar and steel, and the entrances to the crawl space above camouflaged with elaborate overhead lighting systems. Menye had also had peepholes—the kind usually installed in front doors so the occupants could see who'd come calling before opening up—above all of the rooms.

He had retreated up into the crawl space through the hidden trapdoor in his bedroom ceiling as soon as the first shot had been heard downstairs. Then, when the two Americans reached the second floor, he had crawled along the hot, humid and narrow passageway, watching them systematically take out the rest of his guards in the warehouse apartment.

It had mainly been the big man in the torn coat who did the shooting, methodically going first around each corner and leading the way, mowing the Cameroonians down like some robotic killing machine. Menye had to admit the big man was good. He—who Menye guessed was an American—worked almost like the cyborg in the *Terminator* movies. Regardless of what came his way, he killed it and moved on.

Many stray shots—primarily from his own men as they dropped in death—had hit the ceiling. Some had come so close to Menye that he could feel the vibrations. But the bullet-resistant lining had remained intact.

A good half hour had passed since the shooting had stopped and the big American and his partner had left, so Menye finally decided it was safe to pull his cell phone out of his pants pocket. He could probably even come safely down out of the crawl space if he so chose. But he didn't. There was no sense in taking chances before he had more bodyguards around him.

Let the fools carry the guns had always been his personal conviction. They were what the Americans called a dime a dozen and expendable. But members of the intelligentsia, such as himself, were far too valuable to humanity to risk early death.

Tapping numbers into the phone, Menye waited for it to ring. Finally, a husky voice answered in Franglais—a language that was becoming increasingly popular in Cameroon. It was a mixture of French and English—both national languages of the country—with a good measure of Creole thrown in.

Menye found the language irritating. To the former president-dictator, Franglais symbolized a new Cameroon. A Cameroon without him.

"Speak English or French," Menye ordered. "I do not care to listen to the garbled mumblings of young street punks."

"Please accept my apologies," the voice on the other end of the wavelength said. "It is just that so many of our younger guards—guards still very loyal to you, I should add—speak it. I am afraid I have let it catch on inside my head in order to communicate with them."

"Well, Hammid," Menye said impatiently, using the man's name for the first time, "get it *out* of your head, or when I return to power I will see that your head is separated from your body."

"Yes, Mr. President," Hammid said.

"My apartment has been decimated," Menye went on. "All of my men stationed here are dead. I am in the crawl space."

"What!" Hammid shouted into the phone. "What has happened?"

"Two very capable men—Americans, I believe—came through like an Old-Testament horde of locusts."

"Americans?" Hammid repeated. "Were they the Secret Service men we attempted to kill at the airport? The ones whose plane we destroyed?"

"They may have come to Cameroon with the Secret Service men," Menye answered. "But I do not think they were Secret Service agents."

"Might I ask what makes you think this is so?"

"Because they did not look like, or behave like, Secret Service men," Menye said. "Secret Service agents learn to protect people and work counterfeiting cases. These men behaved more like soldiers. Perhaps they are CIA-trained assassins. I don't know." This time when he drew in air, it was through clenched teeth. "In any case, I want them dead. Do you understand me? I want them *dead,* I want them dead *now,* and I want to see their heads on the tips of spears planted in the ground."

"Yes, sir," Hammid said again. "I will send all of the remaining men to hunt them out. We will—"

"You fool!" Menye shouted into the phone. "Have you

forgotten about *me?* I am trapped inside the crawl space above the coffee warehouse. I will need new bodyguards to take me to another of our safehouses."

"Yes, sir, of course, sir," Hammid said quickly. "I meant I would send all of the men who were not coming to get you after the Americans."

Menye gritted his teeth even tighter. Maybe that was what Hammid had meant. Maybe it wasn't. Hammid was not a bad personal protection agent, and was even a good leader of other men. But he came nowhere close to Menye in the intelligence department, and the vacated president found it irritating that he was forced to be served by men of lesser intellect.

Sweat had gathered on the former Cameroonian president's forehead, and he used the sleeve of his shirt to wipe it off his brow. He considered going down to wait for the new men to arrive, but he could still not be certain that the Americans wouldn't come back.

For a brief moment, Menye wondered if it was cowardice keeping him hidden in the uncomfortable crawl space. But as quickly as the thought had entered his mind, it was gone again. He was no coward. He was simply protecting Cameroon's most valuable asset.

Him.

Once this ridiculous emergency election was over and the KNDP and CPU had killed each other off, he would return to the presidential palace amid the clapping of hands and cheers from the crowds. By then the heat, as the Americans called it, would have died down with the International Criminal Court as well. The entire world would be begging him to return to power and rid the country of chaos.

Suddenly realizing that he was still connected to Hammid by the cell phone, Menye said, "Send your best men to get me immediately. And while I have your attention, how did the shooting at the Hilton go?"

"We cannot be certain," Hammid said. "But we believe one of the Secret Service men was hit. Three of them left and were followed to the nearest hospital."

"Were two of them carrying the third man?" Menye demanded.

There was a long pause. "No, sir," Hammid finally said. "They were all walking. But two of them were holding the arms of the third man, and he had a towel wrapped around his head."

"You idiots!" Menye started to scream into the phone. Then remembering the possibility that the Americans might have come back, and that he might be heard, made him change the scream to a whisper. "It could not have been a serious wound if the man with the towel was walking."

"We will try again," Hammid said. "But we will have to come up with a different plan. As I'm sure you will understand, we were forced to vacate the office across the street from the Hilton. We will find some other place to set up. Or perhaps we will infiltrate the Hilton itself."

"I don't care how you do it," Menye growled in a low voice. "Just do it."

Without further ado, the former Cameroonian president pressed the button to end the call.

Lying still on his stomach against the cold steel of the fortified crawl space, Menye could feel that the sweat had soaked all the way through his shirt. Chills went down his spine as he lay there, and he wondered once again if it would be safe to leave this cramped and uncomfortable passage and go back downstairs.

No, he told himself. That would be selfish. It might mean getting killed, and that would not be fair to the Cameroonian people. He was their one hope. Undoubtedly their only hope.

And the feeling he had in his chest and abdomen? The fact that his hand had shaken during the entire time it had held the cell phone? That was not fear—it was adrenaline, he told himself. The kind of adrenaline only a man of his great mental capacity could experience at the thought of once again ruling over his subordinates.

"No," Menye whispered to himself. "It is *not* fear. It is not fear at all." He paused a moment, then took a deep breath. "I am not afraid."

But the feeling in his gut still felt a lot like fear when he pictured the big American again in his mind.

"So," LAREBY SAID. "We've got all of these new toys. But what do we do with them?"

Bolan, Lareby and Antangana had returned to the Hilton, storing most of their equipment in suite 307. Layton Williams and Tom McLaughlin of the Secret Service had done the same in the adjoining rooms. The next task the Executioner had performed was checking to make sure that all of the window blinds and curtains were closed.

McNiel had seen to it right after Robertson had been shot. But Bolan took it a step further, pulling a roll of silver duct tape from one of his bags, then taping the curtains together in the middle and running another length down the sides to eliminate the tiny gaps at the wall.

Bolan closed the doors to the adjoining rooms. An idea had been gnawing at his gut ever since their plane had landed to the hail of gunfire at the airport. The attempted sniping of the Secret Service agent had further confirmed his suspicions.

There was a traitor in their midst. Or at least close enough to alert their enemies of their moves ahead of time. They—meaning any of their potential enemies, the KNDP, CPU, or Menye's supporters—had known exactly which plane would be carrying the Americans. And they had almost wiped them out while they were still on the tarmac.

The sniper, too, was proof of a leak. He had somehow not only known they were staying at the Hilton, he had known exactly what rooms they were in.

Bolan thought about calling down to the front desk and getting different rooms, but he saw little point in doing so. If so much intel had already leaked out, it was likely that the sniper—and the rest of their enemies in Cameroon—would immediately get that information, too.

Bolan took a seat in an armchair and stared at the wall in thought. He was fairly sure that Menye's men had not had advance warning that they were about to be attacked. If they had, they could have simply vacated the premises and taken Menye with them, avoiding any possibility of defeat by avoiding battle. As things were, it appeared that they had sent Menye on to some other safehouse. But if the former president wasn't at the warehouse, why had so many armed men remained there?

It didn't make sense. There had to be more to it.

Bolan didn't know what it was, but he was determined to find out.

For the time being, the best thing he could do was have Antangana contact his snitch again and try to pick up a new lead that way.

Bolan remained where he was as Antangana dropped down on the one end of the couch. The sick man looked as if his eyelids weighed a ton each, and it was obvious that he needed rest. Lareby took another armchair in front of the coffee table. The soldier turned to the prime minister. "Call your informant," he said. "See if he's got any other intel that can get us jump-started again. And put the call on speaker-phone."

The man in the dashiki nodded wearily, and Bolan was

reminded again that the cancer was taking its toll. He was due for another round of chemotherapy soon, and that would drain even more energy from him. As the soldier watched, it took extreme effort on Antangana's part to lift the tail of the multicolored shirt and pull a small rectangular cell phone from the pocket of his slacks. The muscles in his face tensed slightly in pain, and his hands shook as he punched a number into the instrument, then set it on the coffee table in front of them.

A moment later, Bolan and Lareby could hear the rings as the line tried to connect. Then came a click, and a hoarse voice said, "Hello?"

"It is me," Antangana said a moment later. Then he paused to catch his breath. "Menye was not at the warehouse as you told me he would be," he finally got out. "You were wrong."

A long silence followed. Then the voice on the other end of the call said, "Did you check the crawl space?"

Bolan's head snapped toward Antangana. But before he could speak, Antangana said, "*What* crawl space?"

"The one above the ceiling. It runs throughout the remodeled upstairs apartment. I am sure that I told you about it."

Antangana worked up enough strength to say in a loud voice, "And I am sure you *did not* tell me about it. This is the first I have even heard about a crawl space."

"Jean," the hoarse voice said in African-accented English, "I *must* have told you. Menye fortified the ceiling when he turned the second story into a safehouse. The crawl space was a hiding place of last resort, in case the apartment was breached. It was in case of an all-out attack—just like the one which you instigated."

Bolan had continued to stare at Antangana. Now the man's face looked more confused than tired and pained. The question was, had the informant kept that bit of intelligence info to himself on purpose, or had the strong pharmaceuticals which the prime minister was taking for his illness caused a breach in memory? Many drugs, especially those for pain, created memory loss.

But there was a third possibility, as well. This informant might have known that the men with whom Antangana was working would blame the problem on the drugs, which would give the snitch enormous "wiggle room" and allow for giant gaps in the information that he passed along.

That was the downside of using informants. You never knew when they were playing both ends against the middle.

Lareby was already on his feet again. "We ready to go back?" he asked as he unconsciously placed a hand on one of the .45s in his belt.

Bolan didn't move except for shaking his head. "There's no point in it," he whispered away from the cell phone. "Menye will be long gone by the time we get back there."

Turning toward Antangana, he whispered again. "Get a new lead out of your man. Find out where the former president might have gone." He paused for a moment, thinking, then added, "And set up a meeting with this guy. I'm tired of working on intel I get from a man with no face."

Antangana nodded. "We must meet, Paul," he breathed into the phone as he leaned over the coffee table.

"No," the voice said. "And you were not to use my name during these calls."

The soldier had heard enough. He leaned over, and in his strong, angry-but-controlled voice, said, "Your way hasn't worked out too well so far, *Paul*." He put special emphasis on the man's name. "We are going to meet each other. You can come voluntarily, or I can hunt you down. But if I have to do that, I'm going to get all of the information out of you I can, then gut you like a fish and leave you for the scavengers." He paused to let the message sink in, and while he waited, he saw Antangana wince.

"He can be trusted," the prime minister said. "There is no need to threaten him. I am certain of it. And I am certain that he must have told me about the crawl space and the drugs in my system just made me forget."

"Maybe yes, maybe no," Bolan said to the side. Then, into the phone again, he said, "Did you get all that, Paul?"

Several seconds went by during which the only sounds coming over the line were short, shallow breaths. Then the voice finally said, "All right. But we must make it somewhere safe. I cannot be seen associating with Jean. You will understand why when I meet you."

"I know the perfect place to meet," Antangana stated, then specified the location.

11

The road leading to the Ekom Waterfalls was located approx-
imately seventy miles from the city of Douala. Bolan guided
the rented Land Rover through a small village, then deeper
into the jungle. All along the asphalt roads they had encountered potholes and other examples of disrepair, and the vehicles that passed them going into the city all seemed to be
ready to collapse at any moment. Missing fenders, dented
hoods and doors, and ragged tires ready to burst were the
norm for the impoverished country.

The Executioner finally turned off the asphalt onto what
was little more than a jungle pathway. Slowly, he navigated
the Rover through branches, vines and other growth that bent
against their bumper and windshield, then whipped back into
place as they passed. He could hear the falling water long
before it came into view. It had a pleasant, relaxing reso-
nance, a sound at the complete opposite end of the spectrum
from the pressure this mission had dropped on his shoulders.
Not that he wasn't used to it. Every assignment he took on—
whether on his own or by reference from Brognola at Stony
Man Farm—was vital to somebody somewhere.

But that didn't mean Bolan never had time to notice the
beauty around him, and when the twin waterfalls finally

appeared through the thick mass of leaves and jungle vines, he saw that they were no less than spectacular. The two falls, separated by the rock formation behind them, fell about a hundred yards off the mountaintop. The road ended well before the edge of the cliff overlooking the river below, and those same leaves and vines would keep the Land Rover invisible to anyone on the other side, or around them on other roads.

Bolan had killed the headlights as soon as they'd turned onto the isolated road, driving at a snail's pace in what little light penetrated the jungle around him. He threw the transmission into Park and sat back against the seat.

Lareby rode shotgun, and the Executioner watched as the man pulled the slide on one of his Colt Government M1911 .45s back far enough to catch a glimpse of the brass in the chamber. The CIA agent replaced the weapon in his belt, then repeated the process with both his other .45 and the smaller Walther PPK.

Unlike the average television and movie watcher would be led to believe, true warriors did not wait until the last minute to chamber a round in their weapons. They pulled back the slide long in advance, then removed the magazine and topped it off with another round. And on a single-action semiauto like Lareby's .45s, the pistol was carried with the hammer back and the thumb safety on. The grip safety, on the rear of the handle, provided extra insurance that the gun would not go off accidentally in this mode.

Bolan had removed the bulb from the Land Rover's dome light before they left Yaounde, so the interior of the vehicle remained dark as he opened the door, got out and closed it quietly behind him. Opening the door to the backseat, he reached in and grasped a worn-out and napping Jean Antangana by the shoulder, shaking him gently awake.

The man's disease, coupled with what they'd been through already that day, had completely tired him out.

When Antangana's eyelids finally lifted, he looked out at the soldier, frowning, appearing as if he wasn't sure where he was or possibly even *who* he was for a moment. Then his expression relaxed and he turned his head toward the waterfalls, looking at them over the backseat and through the Land Rover's windshield. His eyes tried to close again, but Bolan watched the dying man fight the urge and then say, "Mr. Cooper, if you would help me please…"

Bolan reached in with both hands, practically lifting the prime minister off the seat. It was almost shocking how light the man had become, and that explained why he wore the baggy dashiki to hide his emaciation. A moment later, he was leaning against the rear of the vehicle as Bolan closed the door and Lareby joined them at the bumper.

"I'm not sure I've ever seen a better place for an ambush," the CIA agent said, and Bolan noticed that he already had one of his .45s dangling from his hand.

"You're right," Bolan said. "But it's also a perfect place to meet an informant and not be seen."

Antangana was fully awake, and in the semidarkness of the jungle Bolan watched the man nod. "The two goals often end up in similar places."

"I won't ask you again if you trust your informant," Bolan said in a low voice. "If he was trustworthy, he wouldn't be an informant in the first place."

"How unfortunately true," Antangana said. "But I truly believe that this man has reformed."

"We'll see," Bolan said, and then the three men fell silent. The only sound in the dense jungle around them became that of the waterfalls across the river. They were too far away to make out the details, but among the rugged terrain around the falling water he could barely see the shadowy forms of tourists. Here and there, a flashlight beamed as the visitors took in the spectacular view at night. The fact that there were innocent people on the other side of the waterfalls didn't set particularly well with Bolan. Telling the "good guys" from the "bad guys" on this mission was already hard enough. But Antangana had assured him and Lareby that no one used this isolated road on this side of the water. It ended too far away from the waterfalls to attract sightseers when they could easily get right up next to the falls on the other side.

Ten minutes went by. Then twenty. The three men remained silent until Lareby finally looked at the glowing numerals on his wristwatch and said, "Is he coming or not?"

Antangana knew the question was meant for him, and replied with, "He is often delayed." He held his fist to his mouth and coughed, then added, "He will be here."

No sooner had the words left his mouth than the sound of an engine began to hum from somewhere on the road behind them. As it grew louder, Bolan reached under his arm and drew the sound-suppressed Beretta 93-R. He didn't care for this meeting place any more than Lareby had, but there had been no sense in verbalizing his dissatisfaction.

This was where Antangana had arranged the meeting, they were here, and that was the reality of the situation. They would either have a successful meeting with Antangana's snitch, get killed in an ambush or kill whoever tried to ambush them.

And that was that.

Finally, the dark silhouette of an ancient Ford pickup came to a halt roughly ten yards behind them. Bolan flipped the Beretta's switch from safe to 3-round burst, then reached up and pulled down the collapsible front grip below the barrel and clutched it in his left hand.

A lone figure exited the pickup and walked slowly toward them. As he neared, the man stretched his arms out to his side, his fingers spread wide to show that he carried no weapons. At least not in his hands. His torso was covered by another brightly colored and patterned dashiki similar to the one Antangana wore.

That was a good sign, but not quite good enough for Bolan or Lareby to holster their guns.

A second later, the man stood in front of them, then slowly extended his hand to Antangana, who grasped it with both of his. Bolan was suddenly struck by the similarity of the features of the two men. While an inch or two shorter, the informant actually looked like a stronger, healthier version of Jean Antangana.

"It is good to see you, my brother," the newcomer said.

"It is good to see you, as well," Antangana said, and then the two embraced.

Bolan frowned. "By brother, do you mean friend and companion or blood?" he asked.

Antangana dropped his arms and stepped back. "We had the same mother and father," he said softly, ending that confusion. "But Paul, here, never had any political ambitions as I did. He is basically a mercenary. But in the last few years I have been able to convince him that he should work for the good of Cameroon, rather than whoever paid the most."

"Why didn't you tell us this before?" Bolan demanded to know.

"Because there was no need to tell you before," Antangana said. "And just as you have done with me, I have been hesitant to fully trust the two of you." He stopped talking again to catch his breath, then finished with, "But it appears that we are all satisfied at last that we are on the same side."

"Maybe," Bolan said. He turned to face Paul Antangana's shadowy form. "How is it that you know so much about Menye and his safehouses?"

Jean Antangana answered the question for his brother.

"Paul's cover is that he is a trim carpenter," he said. "Actually, he is quite skilled. Menye hired him to remodel the coffee warehouse apartment, as well as several other houses where Menye planned to hide if things went badly."

"Yet you forgot to tell your brother that the ceiling had been fortified?" Bolan asked with more than a hint of disbelief in his voice.

"Sadly," Paul said, "no. I *did* tell him. His disease has made him forget."

It was too dark to see the expression on either man's face. But the tone of Jean Antangana's voice sounded both embarrassed and sincere. "It is my fault," he said. "I remember something about it now, but the memory is hazy. And I must admit I have forgotten other things I should have remembered because of the drugs, radiation, chemotherapy, or all three."

Bolan felt sorry for the man, but there was no room for sympathy on that front at this moment. "Is there anything else you've forgotten to tell us?" he said, trying hard not to sound angry.

"If there is," Paul said, "I will fill you in as we go." He stopped talking for a moment, then said, "Perhaps it would be better if I stepped into my brother's shoes and accompanied you from here on out."

Bolan remembered how light Antangana had been when he pulled him from the Land Rover's backseat. The man couldn't have weighed more than a hundred pounds.

Antangana was worn out and sick. He needed to return to Yaounde for both rest and treatment. Besides that, everything he had given them had come from this source—his brother. It made no sense to get intel secondhand when it could come straight from the horse's mouth. Besides that, Antangana's on-again-off-again memory might just get them all killed.

"I think you're right, Paul," Bolan said. Before the prime

minister could protest, the Executioner held up a hand. "You've been of tremendous help, but you need to go back and get well."

"I am not going to get well," Antangana said. "Only an act of God could accomplish such a feat."

"Then you need to go back and pray for that act," Bolan said. "You've already gone far beyond the call of duty. You need to—"

The sound of another vehicle coming down the road behind the pickup suddenly stopped the soldier in midsentence. Through the thick foliage he could see headlights in the distance. He turned to Paul.

"Did you bring anybody with you?" he asked. "Any backup, in case you were being set up?"

Paul shook his head vigorously in the dim light.

"Were you followed?"

"I didn't think so...."

"It sounds like you might be wrong," Bolan said. "Which means we're in for a fight." He opened the tail door of the Land Rover and pulled the Saiga 12-gauge semiautomatic shotgun from the vehicle, clipping the 25-round drum magazine to the weapon's receiver.

Automobile lights suddenly shone brightly upon them as Lareby and Paul reached into the Land Rover for long guns.

The first round from the vehicle coming down the dead-end road smashed into the Rover, an inch from the Executioner's face.

12

Dennis McNiel had not seen such an undisciplined group of people since he'd been in kindergarten. The men of the Kamerun National Democratic Party had absolutely no comprehension of order, and as he did his best to speak into the microphone in the Hilton's large meeting room, he saw fists raised defiantly into the air. He noted the hurriedly made cardboard signs with political slogans scribbled on them among the shouting voices.

"Please!" he finally screamed into the microphone. "Will you *please* come to order!"

Next to him, Colonel Essam—dressed in full military dress complete with medals—translated McNiel's words into French, even mimicking the American Secret Service man's disgusted and semifrantic tone of voice. Still, it took a good thirty seconds for the mob to get their last angry words shouted meaninglessly into the air before the room gained some semblance of quiet.

"Listen to me!" McNiel said in a more quiet voice, and Essam translated again. "We are here to help you."

The statement brought more pandemonium, a mixture of cheers and jeers. It was clear that while some of the KNDP representatives crowded into the meeting room were happy to have American help, others were not.

McNiel shook his head back and forth in frustration. Then he cleared his throat and yelled, "Shut the hell up!"

The crowd quieted immediately—even before Essam could spit out the words in French—and it became clear to the Secret Service agent that what he faced here in Cameroon was the same problems he had heard from GIs returning from Afghanistan and Iraq.

No one paid any attention until you got mean. They were so used to being treated forcefully that if you wanted someone to cross the room, you had to grab him by the arms and at least get him started. Otherwise, your words went unheeded.

So Special Agent Dennis McNiel stepped down from the podium and clenched his fingers around the arm of the man nearest the microphone. The man's name was Richard Ayissi. He was the KNDP's presidential candidate, and the seeming incongruence of his first and last name merely symbolized the many divisions of race, religion, tribal and political affiliation found in modern-day Cameroon. McNiel jerked him back up onto the stage and, while the room remained quiet, said, "We, the United States of America's Secret Service, have been entrusted with the safety of your candidate."

It was clear that enough of the KNDP mob spoke English that their reactions began even before the translation.

"We have our own bodyguards!" one man in the middle of the crowd shouted back. "We do not need you!"

"We're working in conjunction with your people," McNiel said.

By this point Essam had translated, and the overall attitude of the men at the meeting appeared mixed. Many appeared to be in favor of using the U.S.'s resources. Others were not. It was a divided crowd, which meant violence could break out between the two directly opposed factions at any moment.

To McNiel, that meant it was time to get the hell out of Dodge. Turning to presidential candidate Ayissi, he said, "Get on the microphone, tell the dissenters you want us with you, then let's get out of here. We're accomplishing absolutely nothing by staying, and we're about a breath away from a full-scale riot rather than a meeting."

Ayissi spoke a few words to another man who had stood near the front of the mob, then turned back to McNiel. "My vice-presidential candidate," he said as the man stepped onto the short stage. McNiel looked back into Ayissi's dark brown eyes.

"Do what I told you to do," he said. "Take the mike and quiet them down." Then he turned to Colonel Essam.

"As soon as Ayissi is finished, you take over," he whispered into Essam's ear.

The colonel frowned at him. "What is it you want me to say?"

"I don't care," McNiel countered as he turned back toward Ayissi. "Just keep them busy long enough for us to get the candidates out of here before anyone realizes what we're doing."

Ayissi spoke softly into the microphone and his words appeared to calm the mob. At least a little. Then Essam stepped up to the podium and placed his hands on the sides of the wood. He began speaking in French and, while McNiel couldn't understand his words, the tone of his voice betrayed the fact that he considered himself to be an extremely important human being.

Regardless, the crowd simmered down even further.

McNiel waited until the rest of his men had escorted the Cameroonian candidates through a break in the curtains right behind him, then out of the back door of the room. He gave them time to get most of the way to the vehicles parked outside the Hilton. Then, with Essam's booming voice growing louder with each word, he slipped off behind the curtain and through the door to the hallway.

All of the vehicles were filled to the top with gas and running when McNiel finally reached them. Sliding into the passenger's seat of the lead car, he noted Ayissi in the middle of the backseat, squeezed in between Fourfeathers and McLaughlin. Without speaking, McNiel wrapped the radio headset from his pocket around his head and spoke into the mike.

"Elvis has left the building," he said, using the prearranged code words they'd come up with before the meeting. "Move out. If they haven't realized we've crept away yet, they will any second. And a lot of those guys are still not in favor of our help."

McNiel nodded to Williams who was behind the wheel of the lead Secret Service sedan, and the agent threw the transmission into Drive. Five other automobiles followed.

The last car had just left as several angry-looking KNDP men, dressed in traditional costumes but carrying very modern AK-47 assault rifles, began pouring out the back of the hotel. But by the time it dawned on them exactly what had happened, all six cars had turned out of the parking lot and onto the highway.

THE EXECUTIONER squeezed the trigger of the Saiga shotgun and a blast of 12-gauge buckshot exploded from the barrel. The blast struck the slanted windshield of the oncoming vehicle and cracked it, then slid up and over the roof of the car, leaving scratch marks in the paint not unlike those some large jungle cat might have left as it crawled over the vehicle.

The second round that Bolan had loaded was a slug. And

another pull on the trigger finished shattering the glass. Even in the darkness, the Executioner watched the round penetrate farther to take off the top of the driver's head as if he'd been scalped down to the nose.

The vehicle—a dark-colored Ford sedan he now saw— veered off the narrow and bumpy jungle road and stalled in the thick limbs and vines to the side. No further gunfire came from the immobilized car.

Pulling out his SureFire flashlight, the Executioner held the Saiga right-handed and kept the barrel aimed at the Ford as he slowly approached. He could see the shadowy outlines of another man riding shotgun, and two more silhouettes in the backseat.

Six empty hands were high in the air above the men's ears.

The Executioner kept the flashlight beam in the shotgun rider's eyes as he cradled it under his arm and opened the door. Reaching into the vehicle, he grabbed the man by the throat and yanked him out and onto the ground, facedown.

Lareby, toting the H&K MP-5, performed a similar act with the man directly behind him. At the same time, Paul— who had produced a giant, four-inch Smith & Wesson 500 Magnum pistol from under his dashiki, jerked the last man from the Ford, on the other side. Paul used the giant revolver to push the man through the thick foliage onto the road, then kicked his feet out from under him with a foot sweep and guided him to the ground next to the other two.

Quick frisks by Bolan and Lareby turned up a multitude of handguns and knives. Paul, in the meantime, recovered four AK-47s from inside the vehicle.

"Paul," one of the men on the ground muttered, "we did not know you would be here."

Bolan looked quickly to the healthier Antangana brother. He was a mercenary. In addition to that, he was Jean Antangana's snitch. Was he also the leak? Was he giving his brother intel about Menye's whereabouts, and at the same time telling the former Cameroonian president's men what his brother and the Americans were up to?

Possible. In fact, *quite* possible. It wouldn't be the first time the Executioner had run into such treachery.

"The question is," Paul said, as he stooped to rest the bull barrel of the 500 S&W Magnum revolver against the back of the speaker's head, "what are *you* doing here?"

Even with the revolver pressed into the back of his neck, the man on the ground shrugged. "We were hired to kill the two Americans," he said.

"By who?" Bolan demanded. "Who hired you?"

"Actually," the man on the ground said, "both sides hired us. Both the KNDP and CPU are paying. But they don't know about each other, and we saw no reason not to take the money from both of them."

Bolan blew air out between his clenched teeth. The whole thing was turning into one royal, complex mess. "Get up," he said.

The men hesitated, surprised, but finally rose to their feet and began trying to brush the jungle mud and the blood from the driver's head off their clothing. Bolan looked at them with disgust. They obviously knew Paul from the mercenary trade. But unlike him, they were still taking any work that came their way, regardless of how immoral it might be.

Bolan was tempted to just shoot them where they stood, but he suspected he could put them to better use alive.

The moon was behind a cloud, and the men's features were barely discernable when the Executioner finally said, "Can I safely assume you've decided against completing your job? Your job of killing me and my partner?"

"Yes, yes, yes," the man closest to him said.

The other two men nodded vigorously in agreement. "We

have already received half of the money from both parties," one man said. "That is good enough for us."

"Good," the Executioner said. "Because the way I see it, you can either help us or I can kill you where you stand."

"We would much prefer to help you," the same man said. "How much does it pay?"

Bolan resisted the impulse to strike the man across the face with the stock of the Saiga. "It pays your lives," he said. He glanced at the near-headless man still behind the Ford's wheel. "An annuity your friend there never had a chance to accept."

"We will gladly take advantage of your offer," the spokesman for the surviving three mercs spit out as soon as Bolan had finished his sentence. "My name is Matak."

Bolan turned to the other two mercenaries. "And your names?" he demanded.

"Amsalu."

"Nijam."

A light breeze picked up from behind the men, and even in the outdoor setting the stench of unwashed bodies blew past the Executioner. He stared hard into the men's eyes, which were unusually bright in the moonlight. He could certainly use their help in finding Menye, but just how far could he trust them? There was no way of knowing.

Matak, Amsalu and Nijam had been quick to accept his offer of their lives in exchange for helping him. They would no doubt be just as quick to return to the other side of this search if it meant money and they thought they could pull it off. And for what he had in mind, he couldn't be with them, watching their every move.

It was a difficult decision, and one which could bring death to Lareby, the Antangana brothers and himself if he made the wrong choice.

Finally, Bolan lowered his weapon and returned to the

Land Rover. Digging through one of the nondescript suit-cases, he came up with three cell phones. He returned to where the rest of the men still stood and gave one to each of the mercenaries. Pulling a small scratch pad and a pen from his vest, he wrote down the number of his satellite phone on a trio of blank pages, then tore them from the pad and handed them, along with a phone, to each of the men.

"You can reach me at this number," he said. "Your job is to get back out there and find out where Menye is hiding." He paused to let his words sink in, then added, "And in case any of you is thinking about just disappearing from me, think again. Each phone contains a global positioning chip which is accurate within a ten-foot radius. It'll also let me know if you've tried to tamper with it."

"But what if it becomes lost?" Amsalu asked.

"Then I'll consider it lost on purpose, and track you down and kill you. You won't even hear it. I'll put a bullet in your head without saying a word. Do I need to get more specific than that?"

"No," Nijam said, speaking for the first time in a voice so high-pitched it almost sounded like a woman's. "I believe we understand."

The Executioner drew the Desert Eagle and pressed the muzzle into Nijam's face. Slowly, he cocked the hammer. Then he turned to touch the big .44 Magnum pistol's barrel to the foreheads of Matak and Amsalu.

"I want you to take a mental picture of this, and store it in your memory," he said in a deep, soft-but-threatening voice. "Because if anything, and I mean *anything* goes wrong, this is the last thing you'll see in this life." He returned the Desert Eagle to his holster as all three of the newcomers nodded in nervous understanding.

"Now pick up your toys," Bolan said as he stepped away

from the pile of guns, knives and other weapons that he, Lareby and Paul had taken from the men.

A moment later, the three mercenaries were armed once more. But now they had a completely different mission. Paul stepped forward.

"Keep in mind," he said, "that I was once one of you. And while you have given our American friends your first names only, I know your last names, as well." He was nodding as he spoke, the huge X-frame Smith & Wesson steady in his hand. "I will easily know how to find you. And find you, we will."

There was an uneasy silence for several seconds. Then Matak said, "So, what do we do first?"

"I'd get that headless horseman out from behind the wheel and get your asses back to what passes for civilization in this country," Lareby said. "The Ford's trashed out a little with that broken windshield. But most of the other vehicles on the roads in Cameroon are in the same shape or worse. You ought to fit right in."

Nijam spoke again in his high squeaky voice. "I am afraid to touch the body," he said. "As I'm sure you know, the HIV virus is rampant all over Africa. If we contract it—"

"Shut up and quit acting like a bitchy little schoolgirl," Lareby said, motioning toward the Ford with one of his .45s. "You've already got the man's blood and brains all over you. If you're going to get the HIV virus, you already have."

"Move," the Executioner ordered, and the three Cameroonian mercenaries scampered toward the car. Amsalu, a broad-shouldered, light-skinned man wearing a blood-soaked white shirt, opened the driver's door and pulled the corpse from behind the wheel. Matak and Nijam helped him drag it out of sight into the thick jungle underbrush.

Paul laughed softly. "We have no need for burials here," he told Bolan, looking up at the taller warrior. "The ants and other insects will take care of that for us. In three days, there will no longer be any trace of the man who was driving the car."

"Get in, and get to work," Bolan ordered the three mercs. He tapped the sat phone on his belt beneath his vest. "Split up and find out where Menye is. And I expect a phone call and update from each of you every hour, on the hour. If anyone misses a call, I'll have to figure you've returned to the dark side. And you know what that means."

By this time the mercs were in the car and Nijam was behind the wheel, looking frightened as he sat in a pool of the driver's blood on the front seat. Bolan watched him touch the steering wheel tentatively, then resign himself to his destiny and grip it with both hands as he backed the automobile, turned and started back down the jungle road.

The Executioner turned to Lareby and the Antangana brothers. "Jean," he said, "we're going to take you home to rest and get your chemotherapy treatments. Paul can take your place."

The prime minister nodded lethargically, too sick, tired and worn out to even argue as his brother helped him into the backseat of the Land Rover.

"What do you want to do with your pickup?" Bolan asked Paul.

"We can leave it here," the man replied. "It'll be found. I stole it right before coming out here to meet you."

The soldier held back a laugh. It was hard to know who was honest and who wasn't under the circumstances, but Paul was not the first car thief he had worked with. And he had stolen vehicles himself over the years when it served the greater good.

Without further words, he slid behind the wheel of the Land Rover, maneuvered the vehicle into a turn and headed down the road leading out of the jungle.

13

Phillip Fourfeathers never said anything about it—that wasn't his way. But in his heart, he resented being called a Native American. He was one, of course, because he'd been born in Oklahoma, which was smack dab in the middle of America. But he knew that the term could be equally applied to people of European, Middle Eastern, Asian, or any other descent who'd been born in the U.S. The simple fact was, his ancient ancestors had come to the Americas from other parts of the world, too. They had crossed the land bridge linking Alaska to Siberia, and probably on boats crossing both the Atlantic and Pacific. "First Americans," in Fourfeathers's mind, was a far more accurate description of his Kiowa and Caddo ancestors, as well as those of his Cheyenne wife, and all of the other people who had descended from the other tribes that had once roamed freely throughout the New World.

Fourfeathers sat backward in the wooden chair, facing the bed in the secluded, bed-and-breakfast-type lodge where Special Agent in Charge Dennis McNiel had chosen to hide Richard Ayissi, the Kamerun National Democratic Party's presidential candidate. The lodge was secreted in a clearing roughly a half mile into the jungle, with only one rugged and bumpy road leading in and out. It consisted of the lodge itself, which contained twenty rooms, and six cottage-style dwellings for people willing to pay a little extra for their "jungle experience." The owner—who had inherited the place when his father died—lived and worked in Yaounde and had let the place run down over the past several years.

Which made it a near-perfect spot to secrete Ayissi. The lodge was no longer on the A list of vacation spots, and both it and the cottages not taken over by the U.S. Secret Service were vacant. Anyone coming down the rough road could be heard and then seen from a distance. That meant that Fourfeathers, his partner and the men from Colonel Essam's protection team could be well-equipped and ready for an all-out war before anyone got close.

The only downside, in Fourfeathers's eyes, was the jungle itself. He didn't know whether it was his Secret Service training, his heritage as a member of the Kiowa-Caddo tribe or just plain old common sense. But his heart told him that if an attack came, it would be from men creeping into the jungle on foot rather than in vehicles.

Fourfeathers glanced back at the bed where Ayissi lay propped up with pillows. Ever since they had arrived, he had been listening to some kind of Middle Eastern/African music that was loud enough to escape his earphones and agitate Fourfeathers. The music was all in the minor key and, to Fourfeathers at least, the voice sounded like the shrieks and laments of a dying man.

Fourfeathers had considered filling his ears with a pair of the spongy plugs he used on the firing range. But the fact was, he needed to stay alert to any suspicious sounds that which might come from outside the cottage. With one eye on the door to the room, the Secret Service agent switched the other from the presidential candidate to his own feet, looking over the burly forearms he had crossed on the back of the chair. The agent wore a pair of plain brown, one-eyelet moccasins that his wife had made. All of the Secret Service agents, as well as Lareby—who he had pegged for CIA, and Cooper, who he didn't have pegged at all—had switched to more casual garb in order to keep from standing out so much in their suits and ties. Fourfeathers had started to change out of his dress shoes into a pair of fancy mocs—also made by his wife—but had decided against it in favor of anonymity. His fancier footwear, which had taken his wife months to cut, sew and bead, had a buffalo on the sides, indicating that he possessed a buffalo spirit. And the waterfowl designs on the top meant he was accepted by the Cheyenne tribe as well as his own Kiowa and Caddo warriors. If he had to pick his two most prized possessions, one of them would be those beaded works of art. But here in Cameroon, they would shout out foreigner. So they were still packed away in one of his suitcases.

He suddenly rose with the grace of a panther. The speed and smoothness of his motion did not come from some sudden threat of danger. It was simply his way. Walking to the far side of the room where the sink, a stove and a refrigerator stood, Fourfeathers opened the refrigerator door and looked inside. The three cold racks were filled with a variety of soda pop cans. Reaching in, he pulled out a Caffeine Free Diet Coke, closed the door again and flipped open the tab. The can made a hissing sound as he returned to his chair.

Ayissi was still listening to his music when Fourfeathers returned. As he sipped the Diet Coke, his thoughts returned to his youth. He had been a high-school All-State defensive end in football, racking up more quarterback sacks than anyone on record. The "Tomahawk" they had called him, and his prowess had earned him a full-ride scholarship to the University of Oklahoma.

But his career had ended abruptly, and badly. During his freshman-year three-a-day August practices, it had been his

turn to hold the blocking dummy and he had let his mind slip
for a moment to watch a dark-skinned cheerleader practicing along the sidelines. At that precise moment, a linebacker
from Midland, Texas, had hit the dummy so hard that it sent
Fourfeathers and the dummy both airborne. He had come
back to earth awkwardly, twisting his right knee, tearing
both cartilage and ligaments, and ending what had all the
earmarks of becoming a successful college career that might
have even led to the NFL.

He took another sip from the can. He never knew whether
to be happy or sad when he thought of that moment. Yes, it
had ended his football-playing days. But the dark-skinned
cheerleader had turned out to be Indian, too, and had made
him those fancy-beaded moccasins while he convalesced
from the ensuing surgery.

Two years later, she had become his wife.

Fourfeathers looked out around the room again. Dwight
Day, his partner on this unusual protection detail, sat on the
other bed next to Ayissi's. A Heckler & Koch MP-5 lay on
the bedspread next to him as he rustled through a three-day-
old *New York Times*. And although he couldn't see them,
Fourfeathers knew that two of Colonel Essam's top snipers
were hidden in the foliage somewhere outside the room. Both
of the men wore camouflage from head-to-toe, and were
armed with long-range sniper rifles with which they covered
the door to the room and the back window in the bathroom.

Fourfeathers tilted his head back and drained what
remained in the can. McNiel, the SAC on this detail, had
decided to go heavy on seclusion and light on firepower with
Ayissi. And just to throw off any would-be assassins, he had
done the opposite with Wirij Motaze, the CNP candidate.
Motaze was surrounded by bodyguards and "boarded up"
tight in suite 309 at the Hilton. There, even the sleeping
Secret Service agents were only a few feet away and ready

to handle any attack which might come. In addition to that, McNiel had sent a look-alike off with Colonel Essam and his men. The convoy would drive around the city and out into the countryside until the election was over in order to further confuse the armed opposition.

Fourfeathers arched his back slightly to stretch the muscles and felt the wooden handle of his knife press gently into his kidney. The knife was a flat, beavertail dagger that had been passed down through his family for five generations. It had worn out seven different leather sheaths over the years, and Fourfeathers currently carried it in a fringed leather scabbard that had been as carefully beaded by his wife as his moccasins.

It was his other most prized possession.

The dagger was in direct violation of Secret Service policy, but that policy did little but make Fourfeathers smile. In addition to the MP-5 submachine gun, he carried a SIG-Sauer .45ACP pistol and two extra magazines in a shoulder rig. And if he ever ran out of ammo and was forced to resort to the dagger, facing a Secret Service disciplinary review board that censored him for carrying an unauthorized weapon would seem like little more than a joke.

He considered his life far more important than any government policy. And if the ancient dagger saved that life, he'd gladly push a broom from then on while he laughed at the ridiculous policy that would have gotten him killed had he followed it.

The Secret Service agent glanced at his watch. It was a simple, twenty-dollar timepiece but it kept perfect time. When the battery ran out, he would chuck it in the trash and buy a new one just like he had done with a half-dozen other such watches during his years with the Secret Service.

The beaded moccasins and the beavertail dagger meant

something to Phillip Fourfeathers. Fancy and expensive timepieces didn't.

Without thinking, Fourfeathers crushed the empty Diet Coke can in his fingers, then dropped it into the wastebasket just behind him. He shrugged slightly, adjusting his shoulder holster so that the butt of the SIG-Sauer moved farther to the front beneath his arm, then leaned forward on his arms again.

He had just begun to relax a little when the first gunshot sounded outside the room. And by the time he had the H&K in his hands, the glass behind the closed curtains was exploding as more automatic rounds penetrated the window and the drapes.

Fourfeathers did as he'd been trained to do. Diving across the room, he grabbed Ayissi by the shoulders and threw him unceremoniously to the floor. For a second, his body covered that of the presidential candidate and he felt the same exhilaration he had experienced every time he took down a quarterback before he could pass.

But this was not a football game. It was a matter of life and death. So Fourfeathers rolled Ayissi beneath the bed he'd been sitting on, then turned toward the window. The earphones through which Ayissi had listened to his weird-sounding music had come off the presidential candidate and now lay on the bed.

Fourfeathers couldn't help but feel at least a small bit of satisfaction when he saw one of the attackers' incoming bullets strike those earphones and send them scattering about the room in tiny bits of harmless shrapnel.

14

Bolan, Lareby and the two Antangana brothers followed their three new recruits down the asphalt road back toward Yaounde. As the moon went down and the sun began to rise, the Executioner's sat phone suddenly rang.

Bolan pulled the instrument from his pocket. "Yeah?" he said into the phone. Dwight Day's voice sounded slightly out of breath. But even before the man had spoken, the Executioner knew what was going on.

He could hear the massive roars of gunfire in the background.

"We're under attack," the Secret Service agent said.

"Location?" Bolan asked.

"One of the cottages at the lodge," Day came back. "With Ayissi."

In the distance, Bolan could see the lights of Yaounde's outskirts. "We're on our way," he said into the phone. "Just keep your man safe until we get there."

"We'll try," an anxious Day said. "But we're really outnumbered."

Bolan disconnected the call, then tapped in the number to one of the cell phones he had given Paul Antangana's mercenary friends. "Pull over onto the shoulder," he ordered as soon as the man answered the call.

Without bothering to respond, the dark Ford sedan pulled to the side of the road and stopped.

Bolan got out of the Land Rover, circled the vehicle and helped Jean Antangana out of the backseat. The man was so weak he could barely stand. Half-carrying him to the Ford, the Executioner guided him into the backseat of the vehicle and then stuck his head through the open window. "You take him in for treatment," he ordered the men. "Then you get busy finding out where Menye is." He paused, meeting the eyes of all three men in turn, then added, "I still expect those hourly updates. And don't forget the GPUs in your phones. You mess with them, or lose the phones, and you die. That's a promise, not a threat."

Without waiting for an answer, Bolan pivoted on the balls of his feet and returned to the Land Rover to slide back behind the wheel. He waited until the Ford was on its way again before looking over the backseat to where Paul sat. "You know how to get to the lodge where they took Ayissi?" he asked.

The ex-mercenary nodded. "Word had leaked out before they even got there," he said.

"So why didn't you tell me?" Bolan demanded to know.

Paul shrugged. "I didn't think of it, and the subject didn't come up."

Bolan shook his head in frustration. There was the leak again. It kept showing up to bite him in the ass every time he thought he had a handle on things. But this was no time to worry about it. They had more pressing business first.

"Then you drive," the soldier said, as he switched places with Paul. "Lareby and I'll do the shooting."

For once, luck appeared to be on Bolan's side. The lodge where the Secret Service men were holed up with Ayissi was only a few miles off the road on their side of the city. Paul threw the Land Rover into gear and took the first jungle path that led off of the asphalt highway. A moment later, they were bumping along the rugged terrain at top speed. Had they not been wearing seat belts, Bolan and the other men's heads would have banged continuously against the roof of the Land Rover.

Fifteen minutes later, they came to a smoother road. In the distance, Bolan could see a clearing and the corner of a man-made structure. The sounds of distant gunfire met his ears as he readied the 12-gauge semiautomatic shotgun, and switched the seat belt from around his waist to the calf of his right leg and tightened it down.

In the front seat, he could see Lareby doing the same thing with his MP-5 submachine gun.

Suddenly, they were out of the jungle and in the clearing, surprising the roughly two dozen men who had surrounded the lodge. The almost constant gunfire that came from both inside and outside one of the cottages had covered their approach, and the faces of the men trying to get to Ayissi looked up in shock.

"Keep driving!" Bolan ordered over the chaos. "Cut a swath right through the middle!"

Paul did as he was told, and the Executioner and Lareby— both hanging out of the Land Rover's windows up to their thighs—began firing.

Bolan tapped the trigger of the shotgun and a load of buckshot nearly cut one of the attackers in two. Right in front of him, he saw Lareby shove the muzzle of his H&K into the chest of a man as they drove by him and unleash a 3-round burst of contact shots.

Blood, bone fragments and pieces of bloody organ tissue flew up and over the Land Rover. The Executioner ducked back into the vehicle just in time to keep from being blinded by the gory mess.

The sudden shock of the reinforcements had stunned the men trying to take down Ayissi. But the initial surprise had worn off, and they turned their wrath toward the Land Rover. Bolan fired more loads of buckshot into the chest of two more would-be presidential candidate assassins as they drove past the cabin where he knew Fourfeathers, Day and Ayissi were pinned down. Lareby took out another.

Paul had seen combat in his life and didn't need to be told what to do. Stomping hard on the brake, he took the Land Rover into a 180-degree skid, then hit the accelerator again. This time, Bolan and Lareby took out assailants on the other side of their vehicle. By the time they had crossed back across the cottage from the opposite direction, the Executioner had thrown shots into three more of the men and Lareby had scored another hit.

Then Paul executed another 180-degree skid and started back again. Bolan and Lareby had taken out the men closest to the cottage during the first sweep, and this time they were forced to twist in order to fire over the roof of the Land Rover. Return rounds began to pockmark their vehicle, and Bolan felt one high-speed rifle bullet swish through his vest and burn the skin on his ribs, just to the side of the shoulder-holstered Beretta. But the burn was the only damage the bullet left.

Lareby was finally proving his mettle by firing 3-round bursts from his 9 mm H&K. He had remained calm, and Bolan could see out of the corner of his eye that the CIA agent was taking careful aim before each burst and making each shot count.

Poise under such life-threatening pressure was one of the attributes of the true warrior. A man was either born with it, or he wasn't. It could be improved upon with training and real-time experience, but it could never be learned from scratch if its seed was not already implanted in a man's soul.

And Lareby had the seed.

Another skidding turn sent grass and dirt flying up over the Land Rover and, for a few seconds, the Executioner and Lareby were blinded by a combination of damp mud and dry dust. But so were the assailants on the ground, and for a moment their blind gunfire was the only noise in the clearing.

Bolan and Lareby didn't waste their ammo like their enemies did. They held fire, waiting, and a second later, Paul had driven them out of the dust storm and back into the open clearing. The soldier saw that more than half of the attackers he had originally spotted were on the ground, dead. A few were still standing, firing from just inside the jungle.

But the majority of the men remaining had fled deeper into the foliage, and every second saw more who were choosing to escape rather than die.

With a good half of the 25-round shotgun drum remaining, Bolan put a double dose of buck into the chest and head of a man wearing dirty khaki pants and a mud-spattered white T-shirt. What fell to the ground was nearly unrecognizable as human.

Lareby took out a gunman who suddenly rose from a kneeling position, slung his AK-47 across his back and turned to run. Three of the CIA operative's 9 mm rounds caught him in the spine, penetrating his chest and exiting to send a gigantic splash of red dripping from the green leaves in front of him. The man fell onto his face. As the life left his body, with his severed spinal cord, his shoulders flopped uncontrollably like a fish just hooked and dropped on land. Finally he died, and all movement ceased.

Just as suddenly and unexpectedly as the Land Rover

had appeared, the gunfight halted. Paul brought the vehicle to a stop, and Bolan and Lareby leaped out and raced toward the front door of the cottage. As they approached, the Executioner could see the wind blowing the curtains back away from the broken glass. The door was locked. But a second after he'd tried the knob, the big Native American Secret Service agent he had met earlier—Fourfeathers was his name if he remembered correctly—twisted it open.

"Anybody hurt?" Bolan asked.

Fourfeathers shook his head, then stepped back and let Bolan, Lareby and Paul enter.

Dwight Day was breathing deeply in and out, obviously still trying to come down off the adrenaline high that had seized him during the firefight. Bolan walked to the space between the two beds and saw a pair of shoes jut beneath the box spring. Reaching down, he grabbed them and pulled Richard Ayissi out into the open.

The man showed no outward sign of injury.

But he was clutching a small round CD player to his chest as if it was some sort of good luck talisman. His eyes looked like those of a deer who had just caught the scent of a hunter hidden in a tree stand somewhere nearby.

Bolan looked to Fourfeathers and Day. He had noted their fire from inside the cottage during the battle, and seen more than one of the attackers drop to their rounds. They were good men.

But this site was burned, as undercover cops would have called it. And it was time to move Ayissi to another location.

"Get your stuff together and let's go," Bolan said. "Right away."

Fourfeathers nodded. "We have another site picked out?"

"Not yet," Bolan said. "We'll take him back to the Hilton for the time being. But I don't want him and the other candidate that close together any longer than need be. In fact, I don't even want them to know the other is nearby while they're there."

Fourfeathers nodded his understanding. "We can keep one of them in 309," he said. "The other in 305. Your suite—307—can act as the buffer zone."

"And we'll get Ayissi—maybe both of them—out of there as soon as we can find suitable places," Bolan said, finishing the conversation. His thoughts turned to Colonel Essam. It had been his responsibility to provide a backup site to hide the men, but he hadn't done so. That meant that at the very least he was incompetent.

"We'll lead the way in the Land Rover," Bolan said, as he started toward the door. "It's got a few bullet holes in it, but so do half of the other vehicles in this country. And it's still running."

"Are you taking Ayissi with you?" Day asked.

"Yeah," Bolan said, pausing at the door to turn and answer the question. "Don't take it personally. It's just that if these men knew where this lodge was, they'll have undoubtedly IDed you and your vehicles as well. The Land Rover hasn't been around long enough to get burned."

Both Fourfeathers and Day nodded again.

Sixty seconds later, the Land Rover—containing Bolan, Lareby, Paul Antangana and Ayissi—led the way to the road leading out of the jungle.

The Executioner expected no more trouble. At least not until they got back to the asphalt mess that passed as a high-way in the poverty-stricken nation of Cameroon.

But his eyes scoured the jungle on both sides of the path-way nonetheless.

THE SUN WAS HIGH in the sky by the time Bolan and the rest of the men pulled into the Hilton's parking lot. The soldier stopped just outside a rear door and waited while Lareby and Paul got out of the Land Rover.

The Secret Service vehicles had pulled in right behind Bolan, and a second later the back door was surrounded by bodies. They shielded Ayissi as he vacated the backseat, and a second later they were inside the building.

As the rest of the men escorted Ayissi to suite 309, the soldier parked the Land Rover. As he walked toward the hotel, his thoughts returned to the three mercenaries he had recruited back at the waterfalls. Matak, Amsalu, and Nijam had been sent to use their contacts to determine where Menye might be hiding since he'd left the warehouse apartment. Until he heard back from one or more of them, it made no sense to drive aimlessly around the city.

But there *was* one thing he could be doing while he waited.

Bolan took the elevator to the third floor and stepped off as the doors rolled open. A moment later, he was inserting his key card into the lock of suite 307 and watching the tiny red light on the mechanism turn green. Twisting the knob, he opened the door.

Lareby, Paul and Fourfeathers stood in the living room of the suite, forming a silent wall between the two presidential candidates secreted in 305 and 309. Fourfeathers was the closest to the front door, and Bolan quietly mouthed, "Do they know about each other?"

Fourfeathers shook his head. "Not yet, at least," he whispered back.

Bolan nodded. "Let's keep it that way." He turned to the corner of the room where he had stashed the innocent-looking suitcases that actually contained weapons, ammo and other battle equipment. From the longest bag, he pulled the custom-made sniper rifle and screwed the sound suppressor onto the end of the Shilen bull barrel. In the same bag, he found a spotter's scope and a pair of binoculars. A ballistic nylon wrist band that closed with Velcro, and held five .243-caliber hollowpoint rifle rounds, went around his lower arm.

"Get me one of the bedspreads," he told Fourfeathers and the man turned and came back a few seconds later with a floral-patterned bedcover.

The Executioner wrapped the rifle in the bedspread, then turned to Tim Robertson who had just come in from the adjoining room where Ayissi had been taken. The young agent's head was wrapped with a white bandage, but a tiny amount of blood had seeped through the cloth and formed a spot. Otherwise, he looked fine.

"What's the plan?" Robertson asked Bolan.

"We're waiting on some new intel at the moment," the soldier said as he handed the spotter's scope to Lareby and the binoculars to Paul. "In the meantime, I'm going to the roof to do a little countersniping if the situation calls for it." He paused for a quick breath, then said, "As soon as the three of us are gone, I want you to open the curtains again. This room only. And make sure you and the rest of the men stay out of sight in the other rooms."

"We'll need more bait than just an empty room," Robertson said.

Bolan nodded. The kid was right.

"How about I walk back and forth every once in a while?" Robertson asked.

"You want to play duck in the shooting gallery, do you?" Bolan asked.

"Not particularly," Robertson came back. He tapped the bloody spot that had seeped through his head bandage. "But I'd like a little payback for this."

Bolan looked the young agent squarely in the eye. What he saw was not hate—just determination. And a desire to see justice done. A desire strong enough that the kid was willing to risk his life again to get it.

Robertson seemed like a good Secret Service agent, and with experience, he showed all of the signs of becoming a great one.

"Okay," Bolan finally said. "But walk fast, and keep your appearances random. You form any sort of pattern and if there's a sniper still watching, you're likely to get it worse than you already have."

Robertson just nodded, the intensity never leaving his eyes. "I owe them one," he said simply.

The Executioner pulled the sat phone from his pocket and tapped in a number.

A second later, just across the room, the front pocket of Fourfeathers's blue jeans began to beep. The big Native American answered.

"Let's keep this line open," Bolan said. "Your first priority is making sure the two presidential candidates don't realize they're only a few feet apart. But some of you can peer around the blinds from the other suites and see if you can spot anyone, too. Just be careful that you don't make enough movements to be noticed and become targets yourselves."

Fourfeathers nodded.

A moment later, Bolan, Lareby and Paul were taking the elevator to the top floor of the Hilton. With the rifle wrapped in the bedspread, the elderly couple who rode with them to the eighth floor paid them no attention. When they finally reached the top, the soldier led the way off the elevator and down the hall toward a door at the end.

A single set of steps led to the roof of the hotel, and a few seconds later the three men had opened another door and were standing on the roof. Bolan held up a hand to stop them.

"We're going to be visible from the surrounding buildings

about the time we get halfway to the edge," he said. "So when you see me drop, you do the same. We'll crawl on to the edge."

"What are we using as a hide?" Lareby asked, using an old military sniper's term.

Bolan looked across the roof toward where the bullet that had struck Robertson had come from. There was a large air duct set about three feet from the short retaining wall that surrounded the top of the building.

"We don't have much to choose from," he finally said. "We'll just have to stay below the wall as much as possible. I'll rig the bedspread from that duct to cover the rifle and most of me. You guys will have to partially expose yourselves in order to use the spotter's scope and binoculars."

He started off across the roof. Then, over his shoulder, he said, "There's always the chance that a sniper will spot us before we spot him and we'll become targets. So if either of you want out, just turn around and go back downstairs."

Bolan dropped to his belly. So did the two men who accompanied him, indicating that they were with him for the long haul.

"This is one of those calculated risks that we have to take," Bolan said as he began elbowing his way toward the retaining wall. "Keep one other thing in mind."

"What's that?" Paul asked.

"Once you're settled, restrict your movement to moving your instruments from window to window. And do it slowly. The human eye picks up horizontal movement easily. Especially if it's fast. And if there's a sniper still here, he's been waiting a long time. He'll be anxious to shoot anything that even remotely looks like a viable target."

Lareby nodded slightly and slowly. "That's the advantage the bad guys always have over the good guys," he stated. "They don't care if they accidentally hit an innocent victim."

He drew in a breath. "We, on the other hand, have to worry about collateral damage."

"That's the reality of the situation," the soldier said. "We didn't make up the rules. And we can't change them, either."

The three men's elbows were raw by the time they reached the edge of the roof. Bolan stayed as low as he could, draping one end of the bedspread over the duct and pulling the other up over his head and down to his eyebrows. The rifle rested with the barrel on the retaining wall, and most likely would not be large enough to draw attention. He would keep the lens cover on the scope until the last minute to avoid reflection from the sun.

Lareby and Paul, however, could not afford to take that precaution. They would have to expose the light-reflecting spotter's scope and binoculars in order to make them work. The Executioner considered trading places with one of them. He was asking them to literally risk their lives, but he had no idea how accurate either one of them would be with the customized sniper rifle. And that had to be his main concern.

Seconds went by, turning into minutes. Then the minutes became an hour. The shot that had grazed Tim Robertson had come from directly across the street, a Ramada Inn that was one story shorter than the Hilton. Bolan's gut told him that hotel was the most likely place for more snipers to set up. No other building in the area had such a clear view of the rooms they had taken on the third floor.

The Executioner didn't know if the snipers would be with the Kamerun National Democratic Party, the Cameroon People's Union, or ex-president Menye. But it didn't matter. Either way, they'd be trying to kill one, or both, of the presidential candidates the Executioner and the Secret Service were trying to protect.

By the time the three men on the Hilton's roof were set

up, the sun had risen high in the sky, shining brightly down on the hotels and other surrounding buildings but hiding occasionally behind a cloud. Beneath the bedspread canopy, Bolan could feel the heat.

"See anything yet?" Bolan heard Fourfeathers's quiet voice over his sat phone's speaker.

Leaning toward the instrument, he said, "Nothing so far. You?"

"No," the agent said. "Thought we had a minute ago, but it was just some old lady looking down at the street. Didn't figure you wanted to shoot her."

"No," he said. "We'll give her a pass. What—"

He was cut off in midsentence by Lareby.

"We've got movement," the CIA agent said. "Directly across the street. The Ramada. Third story down, fifth window from the left."

"I see it, too," Paul said.

Bolan jerked the scope cover forward on its elastic band, then let it fall to the chat on the roof. Leaning forward, he could see something moving in the window Lareby had just pointed out. But the sun was so bright it was impossible to make out what it was.

Then, as if God Himself had ordained it, the sun disappeared behind another cloud and the window became as clear as a high-definition television screen.

The Executioner trained the Leupold VARI-X scope on the window, and saw a bareheaded man leveling a rifle at the lower floors of the Hilton. Without hesitation, he took a deep breath, let half of it out, then squeezed the trigger. It snapped like a dry wooden twig, and the head across the street split open like a dropped watermelon. Without thinking, he drew back the bolt of the single-shot rifle, ejected the empty brass case, and racked another .243 hollowpoint round into the chamber.

Fourfeathers's voice was louder and more distinct over the open line this time. "We've got a second shooter!" he practically shouted. "I can see him from here. Fourth floor, second to the left!"

The Executioner swung the custom rifle that way and saw the mustachioed face of a man squinting into another rifle scope. The scope was so clear that he could make out the muscles in the man's forearm flexing as he began to squeeze the trigger.

Bolan beat him to the punch by what could have been no more than a hundredth of a second. Another head exploded across the street as the sound-suppressed sniper rifle did its job. The Executioner worked the bolt action again, inserting another round.

"Sixth floor, right corner!" Lareby suddenly said.

The Executioner swung the rifle once more and saw a man wearing a turban. His face frowned in wonder, as he lifted it up and away from the rifle scope. Bolan could tell by his expression that he knew something was going dreadfully wrong. But he hadn't quite figured out what yet.

And he never got the chance.

The Executioner aimed at a spot directly between the man's eyebrows beneath the turban. And that was directly where the bullet struck. The white turban suddenly turned red and then flew back out of sight from the window, taking the upper half of the man's head with it.

Then, again as if it had been so ordained, the sun came back out from behind the cloud and turned the windows on both sides of the street into mirrors. But no shots came from across the street. And neither Lareby nor Paul—or the Secret Service men watching through the shades below—saw any more threats.

Bolan waited a full five minutes, letting the sun come and go behind more clouds. But if there were any more snipers in the Ramada, they had given up and disassembled. Speaking into his phone, Bolan said, "Fourfeathers, is McNiel within hearing distance?"

"I'm here," the Secret Service SAC said.

"Send some men across the street to search the rooms," Bolan said. "My guess is that if there were more of the enemy there, they're already gone. But they could have just pulled back to wait until we let our guard down again."

"Roger," McNiel said. "By the way, there's three scruffy-looking guys who showed up right in the middle of the fun to see you. You know them?"

"I know them. Tell them to sit tight. We're coming down."

The Executioner killed the call with the push of a button and stood up, wrapping the rifle in the bedspread again. And this time when they crossed the roof, he, Lareby and Paul did so on their feet.

15

The diversion on the roof had been necessary, but it had gotten the Executioner and the rest of his team no closer to ex-President Menye. Bolan was hoping that Matak, Amsalu, and Nijam had returned with intel that would get them started on the hunt again.

Bolan, Lareby and Paul had barely gotten inside suite 307 when they heard the knock on the door. Lareby was the closest, and he stepped to the side of the entryway and held the barrel of one of his .45s up against the peephole—the CIA agent wasn't taking any chances. But when no bullet came smashing through the wood to strike his gun barrel, he finally peered through the hole. "It's the Three Stooges," he said over his shoulder as he opened the door.

Matak, Amsalu and Nijam, still wearing the same ragged clothes they'd had on at the waterfalls, stepped inside. Without being invited, they took seats on the couch.

"So, have you been successful?" Bolan asked.

"We have, indeed," said Amsalu.

"Then let's go," Bolan said. He turned to Lareby and Paul. "Get your gear ready. They can brief us on the way."

"We'll need at least two vehicles," Lareby said quickly. "Why don't you, Paul and I take the Land Rover and Larry,

Moe and Curly here can drive their car. They can brief us over the phone, and we can stop and get out for a last-minute meeting right before we get there."

"All right. Let's move," Bolan finally said and then turned to McNiel. "You're moving everyone, right?" he asked.

McNiel nodded. "Deerfield and McLaughlin went scouting out other hotels as soon as the gunfire stopped. They just called in—they think they've found two other places. We knew after Tim got shot that they—whoever *they* are—knew about this room. After the snipers you took out a few minutes ago, I suspect they know about 305 and 309, as well." He paused and scratched his neck. "The next logical step would be for them to send a suicide bomber up here. All he'd have to do is get on the third floor and he could take everyone out, and frankly I don't have any idea how we could defend ourselves against that."

Bolan nodded. "No," he said. "You've *got* to move. Sometimes discretion really is the better part of valor. But once you're settled somewhere, let me know where you are." He patted the sat phone in his vest. He, Lareby and Paul grabbed the handles of their suitcase equipment bags and started to wheel them toward the door. But as the soldier drew near the Secret Service leader, he whispered into his ear so no one else could hear. "Don't tell Colonel Essam where you've taken the men." He paused for a moment, then added, "In fact, give him a false site. Say, maybe the Holiday Inn on the next block. I want to see how he handles it."

McNiel immediately understood and knew why. So all he had to do was nod.

Bolan, Lareby and the men Lareby had nicknamed the Three Stooges rolled their suitcases out into the hallway.

U.S. SECRET SERVICE Special Agent in Charge Dennis McNiel watched the six men exit the suite, then looked up at the ceiling, whispering a silent thank-you to God that they were about to desert these Hilton rooms for good. The SAC then walked to the window and gently lifted one of the shades. Hard-looking men—all carrying musical-instrument cases or other forms of luggage—had begun to gather across the street from the Hilton.

The Secret Service man didn't like the looks of it. They didn't look like men who were about to check into one of the hotels before performing a concert. No, the violin and bass fiddle cases made McNiel think more of Al Capone and Thompson submachine guns.

Dropping the blind, McNiel opened the door to suite 305 where Wirij Motaze had been kept. All four of the Secret Service men and Motaze were standing in the living room, ready to go. And all four looked awake, although McNiel knew that this location change had cut into their sleep time.

The SAC smiled inwardly. His men never complained about such things. They knew it came with the job. And while they might not be the fighters that Cooper appeared to be, they were damn good at what they did. His thoughts on the big man going by "Cooper," McNiel wondered who he really was. He had never seen a man as big, strong, tough, or smart as this mysterious leader they'd been given. That he worked for America, McNiel had no doubt. But he definitely got the feeling that the man was a free agent of some sort and not a badge- or credential-carrying government employee. Not a mercenary like the three Cameroonians who would work for whoever paid them, but a man who would only accept assignments given out by the good guys.

Whoever, or whatever, Cooper actually was, he also had a personal charisma that made men like McNiel—known within the Secret Service to be something of a renegade himself—have no trouble following his orders. If the SAC had to sum Cooper up in one word, he supposed that word would be "sincere."

Although there was a lot more to him than just that.

McNiel looked at his men again as all of the faces in the room turned his way. As he pulled his phone out of his pocket and tapped in the number for Colonel Essam, he thought briefly of what Cooper had told him privately just before leaving. The big man, it seemed, had come to the same conclusion that McNiel had.

Colonel Essam was not just a blustering idiot with too many medals and ribbons on his chest. He had to be the leak in the organization that had been giving their enemies advance knowledge of their movements.

McNiel had put Fourfeathers in charge of the men in 305 and had already shared the evacuation plan with the man. As soon as he nodded his understanding, the agent began outlining their plan to move Motaze. Satisfied that it was all under control, the Secret Service SAC moved back through 307 to the door to 309.

As soon as he was in the room with Ayissi, McNiel closed the door behind him, pulled out his cell phone and tapped in the number for Colonel Essam.

Essam answered immediately and McNiel said, "Colonel?"

"Yes," the Cameroonian officer breathed on the other end of the call.

"I'm about to brief my men on the logistics of the transfer," McNiel said. "I'm putting you on speakerphone so you can hear at the same time." He tapped another button, then said, "Are you there, Colonel?"

"I am here," Essam came back. His voice sounded impatient.

"Gentlemen, let me have your attention," McNiel said. "We're going to transfer both candidates to the Holiday Inn down the street." No sooner were the words out of his mouth than the other Secret Service agents started to open their mouths to speak.

McNiel held a finger to his lips and shook his head violently back and forth. His men caught on immediately and their mouths closed. "We can take the alleys all the way from here to the hotel on foot, and be there before anyone even knows what's going on. We've secured temporary rooms on the ground floor, but we'll move higher as soon as we can." Then, talking straight into the speakerphone, McNiel said, "Did you get all of that, Colonel?"

"I did indeed. You will all be on foot in the alleyways. No vehicles will be used." He paused a moment, coughed, cleared his throat, then finally spoke again. "My men will seal off all entry to the alleys from the streets."

If the situation hadn't have been so dire, McNiel might have laughed. The coughing and clearing of his throat were classic indicators that the Cameroonian colonel was stalling long enough to come up with a lie. Such "tells" were right out of the rookie cop handbook.

"Sounds like you've got it, Colonel," McNiel said. "It'll be awhile before we're ready to move. I'll call you back just as soon as we begin the transfer." The SAC hung up.

The expressions on the faces of the other Secret Service men and Wirij Motaze could only be described as puzzled. But before they could speak, McNiel held up his hand.

"It's okay, guys," he said as he looked up from the speakerphone. "Both Cooper and I agree that Essam is the leak. It's more than likely his men who tried sniping the windows, and more Menye loyalists who attacked the cottage where we had Mr. Ayissi. So what I just told him was one enormous pile of bull malarkey. I think the proper term is disinformation."

Most of the faces showed relief. A few still looked confused. "Here's how it's *really* going to go down," the SAC went on. "When we leave this room, Robertson and Maynard will lead the way. Mr. Ayissi, I want you walking close behind them. Deerfield, McLaughlin and I will bring up the rear. Now, I don't want more than six inches between anyone. And I want Mr. Ayissi totally shielded. Is that clear?"

He waited while all the heads, including Ayissi's, nodded their understanding.

"We'll proceed that way to the stairs. *Not* the elevator. Robertson and Maynard will open the door, then Deerfield, McLaughlin and I'll leapfrog to the front and you two will take the rear—behind Mr. Ayissi." His eyes moved to those of the other men, making sure each had understood every word he'd said. "There are three vehicles waiting for us outside the back door closest to the stairs. When we open that door, we leapfrog back to the original positions. Remember—Mr. Ayissi is always completely covered by our bodies. Clear?'

"Clear," several low voices answered around the room.

"We're going to have to rely on secrecy rather than firepower," McNiel went on. "Robertson and Maynard will take the lead vehicle, a banged up green Chevy. The middle vehicle—the one that will carry Mr. Ayissi—is a white Nissan. I want Mr. Ayissi in back, on the floorboards and out of sight. Deerfield and McLaughlin will be in the front seat. Deerfield, you're the better driver, so you take the wheel."

McLaughlin looked at Deerfield, then pushed his sunglasses up on his nose with his middle finger. Deerfield got the message and smiled.

"I'll take the last vehicle myself. It's a panel truck with phony Ace Refrigerator Repair signs on the doors. And it's big enough to hold everybody in case things go south on us. Everyone got it?"

Again, McNiel heard murmurs of assent.

"What's our destination?" Deerfield asked.

"We're going back to the same cottages where we were before. We've already got the terrain mapped out, and it's unlikely anyone will think that 'lightning will strike in the same place' again. But this time, we'll have both secrecy *and* firepower on our side." McNiel folded his cell phone and dropped it back into his pocket. Essam was not as incompetent as he appeared. In fact he had hidden his attacks on both candidates behind a veil of stupidity. He was a Menye supporter through and through, and he had pulled it off so skillfully that it had taken the keen eye of Cooper to see through it.

McNiel wondered for a second if he might be able to recruit Cooper for the Secret Service. But his gut instincts told him the man worked alone, and liked it that way.

Looking back up at the agents surrounding him, he said, "Everybody got their vests on and steel plates in?"

All of the heads nodded.

McNiel's eyes focused on Ayissi. The Secret Service SAC was roughly the same height and build as he was. "Mr. Ayissi," the SAC said, "come with me for a minute." He turned, opened the door to the adjoining suite and ushered Ayissi in before following. As soon as the door was closed, McNiel said, "I want you wearing a vest, too." He pulled one of his backup vests out of a suitcase and inserted the steel plate over the heart. "These vests won't stop most rifle rounds, but they'll sure slow them down. So I still want you down on the floorboards in the backseat as soon as we reach the cars."

As soon as Ayissi had the vest on, McNiel left him and walked through the middle suite to the other room where Fourfeathers already knew what was going on.

"You've talked to Essam?" McNiel said.

"Just got off the phone," the agent said. "He said he'd just spoken to you."

"And you told him…?" McNiel asked.

"That we'd be on foot, heading the opposite way as you, toward the Best Western three blocks away," Fourfeathers said.

McNiel looked around the room. "Is everyone ready?" he asked.

All of the heads nodded.

"Then let's move out," McNiel said. "And be prepared— there'll almost definitely be some shooting on this leg of the assignment."

A moment later he was following the other men out the door to the hallway.

16

When they had reached the bottom of the Hilton's stairs, Bolan opened the door at the back of the lobby and ushered the other men through. Then he stepped out and looked past them, through the glass doors and walls to the sidewalk in front of the hotel. Several men had gathered outside holding luggage when he, Lareby and Paul had entered not too long ago. The men had all carried some kind of baggage that Bolan suspected held weapons. But during the short time he had spent with the Secret Service agents, the number of men outside had doubled. They, too, each carried a suitcase or musical instrument case. But these were not the men who had caught the soldier's attention.

It was the one man standing outside who carried *nothing* in his hands.

The rest of the men had gathered around him. Some of them spoke to the man while others looked upward toward the heavens as if praying.

It took Bolan a moment to process the sight and what bothered him about it. But as soon as he realized it was this new man's empty hands, he felt the adrenaline course through him.

The man who had drawn Bolan's attention was of average

height but gaunt, as if he couldn't scrounge enough to eat in war-torn Cameroon. He wore a safari vest similar to the Executioner's own, but it was zipped tightly up to his neck. The vest, which was a good three sizes too large for the man, was nevertheless stretched to the limit, threatening to burst, and defying his thin arms, drawn face and the skinny legs in his tight straight-legged blue jeans.

The bottom line was that the man's midsection .didn't match the rest of his body.

Lareby had stopped next to Bolan, and the three mercenaries stood on his other side. "I think we've got trouble," Bolan said quietly to Lareby.

Lareby had spotted the man, too. "Right here in River City," he agreed, stealing the line from the old Broadway show *The Music Man*.

Before they could move on, one of the other men outside opened a glass door and the man in the tight vest walked in. He seemed to be in some kind of trance, staring straight ahead at the elevators at the back of the lobby near where Bolan and the other men had exited the stairwell. It was as if he couldn't see them at all as he strode purposely toward the elevators that would take him up to the upper floors of the hotel. Bolan frowned, trying to get a look at the man's hands, but they were hidden inside the hand-warmer pockets of the vest.

"I'm going to walk past him," Bolan whispered to Lareby. "If I make a move, you go for his hands. Get them out of the pockets and see what he's holding."

"I think we both already know what he's holding," Lareby said as a bead of sweat ran down his forehead to his cheek. He wiped it off with a forearm as Bolan started toward the man.

The soldier purposely avoided eye contact with the skinny-fat man as he started toward the front of the lobby. But the second he had passed, his head swiveled back around to the armholes in the vest. Yes, the vest *was* too large for the man. And through the gaping holes beneath the man's armpits, the Executioner saw the top tips of several sticks of dynamite. Although he couldn't see them from the angle at which he stood, Bolan knew there would be more dynamite beneath his other arms and probably across his chest and back.

Bolan had stopped as the man walked on. He had no doubt that this suicide bomber gripped a detonator in one of the hands hidden in his vest pockets. So how was he supposed to get it away from this man without giving him time to detonate the dynamite? It seemed impossible.

The would-be suicide bomber was nearing Lareby, as a thousand thoughts rushed through Bolan's brain. If the detonator required a numbered code to set off the dynamite, the man would have to pull it out of his pocket to see the numbers. But if it was only one simple push of a button that ignited the explosion, he could do that without ever exposing his hands.

The soldier glanced around, seeing dozens of men and women coming and going. Then he turned his attention back to the man in the vest. He was heading for the third floor— of that, Bolan had no doubt. But he would not require entry into any of the suites to succeed in his mission. He could simply stand in the hallway and take out the three suites and most of the rest of the floor. So allowing him to get on the elevator was simply not an option.

But if Bolan forced his hand here, and it was a one-punch detonator, he'd kill everyone in the lobby. The Executioner didn't worry about himself. He had faced death too many times over the years and expected a violent death someday. And if this day was that day, then so be it.

Lareby, he knew, understood the dangers when he first joined the CIA. And if the three mercenaries didn't realize that risking your life was part of their chosen profession, they should have. But the other people in the lobby had not signed up for "battle pay." Yet if Bolan failed in the action he had to take within the next few seconds, they would die.

The bomber was almost to Lareby when the Executioner turned fully back around. It was either a number-coded detonator or a push button, which meant he had a fifty-fifty chance of neutralizing the man without blowing up the lobby.

As he upped his pace to catch up with the man in the vest, Bolan saw Lareby move smoothly into his path and grab both of the man's wrists. Bolan drew the thick-bladed TOPS Loner fixed blade from the back of his pants and raised it high over his head. All other movement in the lobby had stopped as people saw the fracas break out, with the CIA agent trying to jerk the other man's hands out of his hand warmer.

The man screamed something in Arabic as Bolan dived through the air, the Loner clenched in a reverse grip. As he collided with the bomber's back, he brought the blade down with all his strength and heard the crunch of bone as the reinforced tip penetrated the man's skull. All four and a half inches of steel drove on into the brain, and as all three men fell to the lobby floor, the Executioner pumped the Loner back and forth to destroy the bomber's ability to send messages to his hand.

A few gasps came from around the lobby, then the screams of both women and men filled the air. Bolan pried the blade out of the bomber's skull to more crackling of bone. Quickly, he wiped the blade on the back of the man's vest, then turned the man over.

"Murderers!" shouted a high-pitched female voice. Lareby had finally gotten the dead man's hands free and the soldier saw the detonator he had only imagined before.

It was not a coded detonator. Just a simple on-and-off switch. If Bolan had not scrambled the correct part of the bomber's brain, they all would have been floating through the air in pieces.

"Murderers!" the same voice shouted out. "Call the police."

Bolan unzipped the vest. A collective gasp came from the crowd when the people saw a good two dozen sticks of dynamite strapped to the man's body.

There were no more accusations of homicide.

Bolan cut all of the wiring between the detonator and the dynamite with the Loner, then slid the blade back into its sheath at the small of his back. He stood up and looked immediately behind him. The men who had been standing around the front of the Hilton had vanished, no doubt expecting an explosion and wanting to get beyond its reach before it happened.

Unlike the man who lay on the floor with the inside of his head scrambled into the Executioner's version of a lobotomy, they had no plans to die for their former president.

Bolan no longer had any doubt who was behind the various attacks on the Hilton. It was not the CPU or the KDNP.

The attackers, all along, had been Menye loyalists. And when Essam had alerted them to the fact that *both* candidates were in the hotel at the same time, Menye had perhaps seen a way to take out all of his competition with one explosion.

Before officials with questions could arrive to impede the transport of the presidential candidates, Bolan led his men back out of the lobby door to the alley where their vehicles were parked. While the Secret Service delivered the candidates back to the cottages, Bolan knew he had only one mission left.

He was going to find ex-President Robert Menye. And while he would do his best to take the man alive so his sins could be publicized around the world as a deterrent to other would-be tyrants, if that proved impossible, he would kill him.

"MENYE IS in a house on the second of two small lakes south of the city," Matak said into the open line between his cell and Bolan's sat phone. "It is in pastureland, owned by one of the largest lumber and cattle dealers in Cameroon. The man is Menye's friend."

From behind the wheel of the Land Rover, Bolan could see the banged-up Ford just ahead of him. In the backseat, Matak had turned to face the vehicle following him.

"Has he used this house before?" Bolan asked.

"Yes," Matak said. "It is a little like your own president's Camp…" His voice trailed off. "The place where your president goes to rest. What is its name?"

"Camp David," Bolan said. "I assume it'll be well-guarded?"

"As well as it can be," Matak said. "May I remind you that Menye has many men who are still loyal to him."

"I think the suicide bomber pretty much convinced me of that," Bolan said.

The soldier could hear Matak's wheezy breathing over the line from the car ahead. "Some are openly with him, others are still in the military or other parts of the government and protect him behind the scenes. In any case, you will have to be very careful in how you approach the house. While there are woodlands that run near land, there is little to no cover for a good half mile around the site itself. Guards will surround the house, and there will be other guards who are stationed at the two gates." He paused again for breath, and Bolan could tell that the man suffered from asthma.

"Are you going to take them with us when we hit the house?" Lareby asked.

"I haven't decided yet," Bolan said.

Paul, in the backseat, cleared his throat. "I do not like saying this because these were once the kind of men I worked with. But if you let them out of your sight at this point, I think there is a good chance that they might go behind your back and alert Menye and his men in the hopes of getting a reward."

"That's exactly what I was thinking," Bolan said.

Soon they were driving down a rugged asphalt highway that wouldn't have even passed inspection as a country road in the United States. Coffee plantations flew past on both sides of the Land Rover, and the sun had began to fall in the sky. The surrounding countryside took on a brownish-gray, and somewhat menacing tone. Bolan and Matak kept the line open, and the soldier could hear the occasional wheeze come over the air.

Fifteen minutes later, twilight had fallen as they passed through a small village. Although the only light came from lamps and lanterns inside the huts, they could see men and women still going about their business, ending the day's work and returning toward their humble homes. Mixed in with the people were a few lowing cattle, clucking chickens and barking mongrel dogs. As they passed through, here and there, the soldier could see the remains of huts and some larger, more substantial buildings that had been burned.

Racism between the tribes, political parties and terrorist organizations never ceased in Cameroon, and genocide was ongoing.

Bolan could only hope and pray that what he, Lareby and the U.S. Secret Service agents were doing might change all that.

A mile or so past the village, they turned a sharp curve on the asphalt and saw a fork in the road.

"Take the left," Matak half gurgled over the cell.

Bolan had noticed early on that Matak was the so-called

alpha male of the trio Lareby kept calling the Three Stooges, but why he didn't give his phone to one of the others who had more wind than him was a mystery. It had to be that Matak felt he needed to keep control over every aspect of their work or lose his position as leader.

It was dark by this point, but a three-quarter moon continued to cast its eerie light over the road. A hundred yards or so after they had taken the left fork in the asphalt, they turned onto a rough washboard road and began bouncing over the packed dirt. Matak came back on the line.

"We will need to hide the vehicles soon," he stated.

"You know the area," Bolan said. "So find us a place."

Matak wheezed again, then Bolan could hear him speaking to Nijam, who was driving. But he couldn't make out the words.

A few seconds later, the red brake lights on the back of the Ford came on, and the lead car turned onto a path. Barely visible in the moonlight, anyone who didn't know about it ahead of time would have missed it. Bolan tapped the Land Rover's brakes, and followed the three mercs off the washboard onto a cow path. A hundred feet or so later, behind the foliage along the road, the Ford's headlights illuminated an old, abandoned one-room frame shack.

Both vehicles pulled around to the back of the crumbling shanty, turned off the lights and killed their engines.

Bolan, Lareby and Paul exited the Land Rover. As the bright moon shone down on their heads, the soldier rummaged through one of the suitcases until he found blacksuits for himself, Lareby and Paul.

The three men from the Ford got out and walked back to them.

"Are we to wear these combat suits, too?" Nijam asked.

"No," Bolan said simply as he and the other two men began changing into theirs.

All three men let out their breath at the same time. "Then that means we do not have to go on with you?" Matak asked.

"No," Bolan said. "That's not what it means at all. You're going with us to show us the way. But you're wearing your civvies in case we need someone to pass for noncombatants at some point."

The disappointment was evident on the three men's faces. "Then we will get our weapons," Nijam said and started back toward the Ford.

"Wrong again," Bolan said as he zipped up his black-suit, put on his pistols and reached into the back of the Land Rover for the Saiga-12 shotgun. "You'll be unarmed."

"But we could be killed!" Amsalu blurted out.

Checking to make sure the 25-round drum magazine of 12-gauge buckshot was filled and ready, the Executioner searched through the bag it had been in until he found a long, cylinder-shaped object. Custom made for the shotgun by Kissinger, he began screwing it onto the end of the Saiga's barrel. "Silencing" a shotgun like that was an impossibility. But Kissinger had managed to tone the volume down considerably, and the device made the 12-gauge blasts sound more like distant thuds of thunder than gunfire.

"Yes, you getting killed if you go with us *is* a distinct possibility. But if you refuse to go, getting killed will be a certainty." He turned the semiauto shotgun toward Matak. "You understand me?"

All three mercenaries nodded.

The Executioner turned to Paul. "Search them for any hidden guns or knives."

The former merc quickly frisked the three men and found one old and rusting .38, a fairly well-kept Browning Hi-Power, and three more of the Okapi knives that everyone in the country seemed to carry.

Bolan turned off his sat phone and made sure the three mercs killed their cell phones, too.

"You lead the way," he told the men. "And if I get even the slightest inclination that you're turning on us, all you'll hear is the sound of a heavy sack falling flat on a concrete floor. And that sack will be you."

Matak, Nijam and Amsalu nodded again. They turned and took off, slowly making their way through the thick trees and vines, their course paralleling the washboard road they had just left. After roughly thirty minutes, the party came to a crossroad and stopped.

Matak turned to whisper to Bolan. "We are at the edge of the trees," he said. "If you will take the lead for a moment, you will see the first of the two entrances to the lakes. And there are guards."

The Executioner moved silently through the foliage until he could look out between the leaves and limbs to a sign above another road leading on. Twin Lakes it said in English, and three heavily armed men stood to each side of the entrance. All six carried AK-47s, which hung loosely on single-spot slings, with pistols holstered on their belts. Bolan turned back to Lareby and Paul.

"Stay where you are," he whispered. "I've got to take these guys out before they have time to realize what's going on." Then, without waiting for a response, he turned back and moved to the very edge of the wooded area.

Bolan leaned against a tree, training the luminous sights of the Saiga on the closest man to the right of the road. The guards were scattered, but all were between twenty and thirty yards away. Perfect for the Saiga. In the shadows, in addition to their handguns, he could see walkie-talkies hanging from each man's belt.

He knew he not only had to kill these men before they spotted him, he had to get it done before any of them could sound the alarm via radio and alert Menye and the men who would be farther on guarding the lakehouse.

A single press of the trigger sent a blast into the chest of the man closest to Bolan. The same thud he had heard when testing the Saiga's sound suppressor on the Stony Man Farm firing range muffled the device. But by then, the Executioner had swung the weapon slightly to the left and was pulling the trigger again. Another thud sounded and a man wearing khaki uniform pants and an OD green T-shirt took the blast in the upper chest and neck. He let out a long, mournful cry as he fell to the ground.

A third shell of buckshot struck the last man on the right. His long hair was braided into dreadlocks, and they splayed out from his head as he went down on top of the moaning gunman already on the ground.

By then the men to the left of the roadway knew something was going on. Bolan stepped out of the trees and fired three more rounds of buckshot as fast as he could pull the trigger. The fourth and fifth guard had barely begun to raise their rifles by the pistol grips when the Saiga ended their lives. The remaining guard had raised his rifle to fire back into the woods.

A telltale 7.62 mm round going off in the night would carry to the house and alert Menye and his men just as easily as a radio transmission.

Had the final guard been a half-second faster, he might have lived as well as alerting the lakehouse. As it was, the sixth 12-gauge load of buckshot destroyed his dark green BDU shirt, the skin beneath it, and the heart and lungs under that.

Bolan hurried forward, jerking the magazine from his weapon and replenishing the shotgun shells in the drum from a pocket in his blacksuit. Behind him, he could hear the feet of Lareby, Paul and the three mercenaries. He stopped, making certain that all of the guards were dead, then joined Lareby and Paul in pulling the walkie-talkies from their cases on the men's web belts. Bolan, Lareby and Paul each kept one of the handheld radios to monitor. But when Matak reached for one, Bolan threw it and the other two out of sight, across the road into the trees.

"You won't need them," he said. "As long as you're with us and behaving yourselves. The same goes for the rifles."

Lareby and Paul joined the Executioner in breaking the stocks from the rifles, then throwing the pieces after the walkie-talkies.

Ahead, Bolan could see the moon shining brightly off of a small lake. The road twisted around the sparkling water, then rose up a hill before disappearing on the other side. Here and there in the moonlight, Bolan could make out what looked like shiny railroad tracks running along the top of the hill.

"What are we facing next?" he asked Matak.

"We must go over the railroad tracks that cross that hill," the merc said, pointing ahead. "This is the smaller of the two lakes. The house is on the other side. On the larger body of water."

"Will there be guards along the way?" Bolan asked.

"I don't know," Matak said. "But after all that has happened, you can be assured that Menye's most capable men will be at the house.

Bolan listened to the man's words. They were about to face the very best of the Cameroonian soldiers still loyal to the former president. And the Executioner's best guess was that they would include Colonel Luc Pierre Essam. The colonel had had a sweet ride so far, pretending to guard the presidential candidates along the outer perimeter while, in actuality, feeding information to the assassins from both the CPU and KDNP in order to get Menye's competition killed.

And, of course, doing his best to put Bolan, Lareby and the two Antangana brothers in the ground at the same time.

"If you don't know whether there'll be more guards before we reach the cabin," the Executioner said, "then we proceed as if there are. I'll take the lead." Jerking the sound-suppressed Beretta from his shoulder holster, he handed it to Lareby. "Trade me for one of your .45s."

Lareby understood what was happening. This exchange would leave both him and Cooper each with a more quiet weapon. He took the Beretta, handing over a .45 in return. Bolan stuck the pistol in the shoulder holster where the Beretta had been. It wasn't a perfect fit. But it would hold. He looked to Paul, who had brought one of the H&K MP-5s with him in addition to his giant S&W 500 Magnum revolver.

"Paul," he whispered, "don't fire until you absolutely have to. We want to get as close to the house as we can without getting seen."

Paul nodded.

A moment later, Bolan and Lareby were leading the way down the road toward the hill and the railroad tracks.

And wondering just what they might encounter along the way.

17

The land slanted steeply down to the lake from the railroad tracks atop the hill, and Bolan sent his men crawling down one at a time, while watching the house at the end of the lake through a set of small night-vision binoculars from a case clipped to his web belt. Far in the distance, he could see men through the sliding glass doors and glass wall that faced the lake. None seemed to take notice of the invaders making their way down to the lakeshore.

When the other five men had crouched next to the water, Bolan rose from where he'd lain atop the hill and rolled down the side to join them. Looking to the three mercenaries he'd captured, he said, "You guys go to the other end of the lake. Give us ten minutes, then start raising Cain."

"What do you mean by 'raising Cain'?" Amsalu asked. "Shooting guns?" He licked his lips in anticipation of getting a weapon.

Bolan had no intention of giving him a firearm. Reaching into one of the pockets of his blacksuit, he pulled out a small can full of lighter fluid and a box of matches. "Pile some wood up and then pour this over it," he said. "But don't light it on fire until the ten minutes are up. Hold out your arms. All of you."

Amsalu, Matak and Nijam extended their arms and then synchronized their watches with Bolan's. "The time starts…" said the Executioner, "*now*." He dropped his arm and turned toward the house as the three unarmed mercenaries took off in the opposite direction.

Bolan led Lareby and Paul along the shore, first to one group of trees, then the next. So far, they had seen no signs of perimeter guards. But when they silently approached the next set of saplings just to the side of the lake, the Executioner made out the silhouette of a man sitting with his back to the trees.

The barrel of some kind of assault rifle was also visible, pointing straight into the air.

The Executioner stopped and held up his hand for the other two men to do the same. Then, creeping closer, he heard the quiet snoring of the man asleep at his post.

Bolan drew the Loner as he entered the trees. His plan was to hold one hand over the man's mouth and slit his throat.

But just as he was bending and reaching for the man's face, the guard woke up. Seeing Bolan face-to-face, his arms floundered wildly in the air, knocking the knife from the Executioner's grasp. Then the butt of the rifle came around toward Bolan's face and, boxed in within the thick trees as he was, the big American was forced to block it with his forearm.

The Executioner knew he had to kill this man, and he had to do it fast. He was too close to the cabin to use the muffled shotgun—it wasn't muffled *that much*. And the Desert Eagle and Lareby's .45 would draw just as much attention.

Remembering the North American Arms Earl he had picked up from the airplane's stores, he jerked it out of one of the pockets of his blacksuit, then jammed the tiny hole at the end of the barrel hard into the guard's throat. The man's own flesh lowered the .22 Magnum round to a hissing sound, and the Executioner pushed the tiny single-action revolver just as hard into his heart.

Another hiss and they were on the move again.

Lareby and Paul moved up into the stand of trees to join Bolan. From that position, they could see the cabin. They were only a football-field length away from the house, but the trees that provided their cover would be the last they'd have.

The only plausible attack was a sudden sprint toward the house. From where he squatted, Bolan could see Menye's guards circling the house, each heavily armed. They'd be lucky if they got halfway to their target before being spotted.

The Executioner looked down at the luminous dial on his chronograph. They had two minutes left before Paul's former associates would light the fire.

Bolan stared at the house. A long porch facing the lake ran the entire length of that side of the building. Several wooden chairs were visible, as well as a rope hammock that had been hung at the end closest to the trees. Some of the guards were lounging along the rough cedar porch, but it was impossible to make out their features—even with the night-vision binoculars. One of these men might be Menye himself. On the other hand, the former Cameroonian president was more likely to be hiding inside.

Bolan's eyebrows furrowed in both anger and concentration. This time, he would not forget to check the ceiling if he didn't find Menye in another room of the house.

The mumbling sound of voices suddenly came from the porch. Bolan looked over his shoulder to the other end of the small lake and saw a flicker of fire. A moment later, a giant gust of flame exploded across the waters, and the men on the porch jumped to their feet, aiming their rifles at the light.

Bolan took off, sprinting up out of the trees with Lareby

and Paul a step behind him. In the darkness, and with the distraction of the sudden fire, he had crossed close to sixty yards before he caught the attention of one of the men on the porch. The man shouted something indiscernible and tried to swing his AK-47 Bolan's way.

He never got it done.

The Executioner lifted the shotgun barrel and tapped the trigger as he continued to run. The first shell full of giant buckshot blasted through the chest of the man who had seen him, and sent him crashing back through one of the sliding glass doors into the lakehouse. By then, Bolan had covered another twenty yards, and his next 12-gauge explosion was from less than five yards from the porch. Close enough, at least, that a few drops of residual blood fell over his hair and shoulders.

The man he had just shot had held a Heckler & Koch 91 in his hands, and the shotgun blast blew the weapon up against his face, the barrel leaving a bright red line across his cheek where it hit.

Bolan took off on his right foot, leaping the four feet or so up and onto the porch of the house. The man in the hammock was starting to sit up when another load of buckshot hit his lower abdomen and chest. He resumed his lying position as the white rope of the hammock turned crimson.

Behind him, the Executioner could hear Lareby firing his M-16 and Paul going to work with his MP-5. The guards along the porch—as well as those to the sides of the house who were coming around toward the lake to join the action—began falling like dominoes to the shotgun, rifle and submachine-gun fire.

When every man on the porch was down, the Executioner looked over his shoulder and shouted, "Take the sides! We'll meet in the front!"

"Where are you going?' Paul asked as he squeezed off a blast of 9 mm rounds from his subgun.

As he let up on the trigger, Bolan yelled, "Right through the middle."

The fire outside the house continued as the soldier stepped into the living room. There was no need to open a door—the glass doors and wall had all been shot out and nothing but sharp shards clung to the edges. Six men stood inside, and the Executioner pumped 12-gauge rounds into two of them before the others could aim his way. Seeing that there was no way to take out the remaining four before at least one of them got him, Bolan dived to his left behind a counter that led into a small kitchen. Rifle and pistol rounds followed him as he hit the tiles, blowing past him to create gray-edged holes in the refrigerator and stove standing against the wall.

Bolan leaned around the edge of the counter and pulled the trigger twice. The next shell to leave the 25-round drum blew the face off a guard wearing spiffily pressed khaki BDUs. He fell back into a reclining chair. Except for the fact that he no longer had eyes and was covered with blood, he looked like a man who might have just settled in to watch a football game.

The Executioner's second pull of the trigger sent more 12-gauge buckshot into the upper chest and throat of a guard with an Uzi. The man staggered backward a few steps, then raised the barrel of the Uzi toward the ceiling. His index finger clenched in death, and he ran the Israeli-made weapon dry. But every bullet that came from the Uzi's barrel went harmlessly into the ceiling.

Bolan ducked back behind the counter as return fire came after him. The multiple rounds tore a hole through the front of the stove and blasted the refrigerator hinges completely off the door. As soon as it died down, the soldier rose over the counter, squeezing the trigger of the 12-gauge and downing the last two men in the living room. Satisfied that no living enemy was still in the front room of the house with him, the Executioner stood up and moved toward what appeared to be a hall door.

Stopping at the edge of the door, Bolan risked a quick glance around. The hallway was empty, except for two sets of bunk beds along the wall. The bedspreads were short enough that Bolan could see below them. No one was hiding there.

With the Saiga leading the way, the Executioner went slowly down the hall toward what appeared to be a small bedroom. To reach it, he would have to cross another connecting hallway.

The soldier stopped at the corner, dropping to a knee and inching an eye around the rough-hewn wooden wall. A man wearing a Cameroonian full-dress uniform but holding another Uzi stood in the doorway to the last room of the house, obviously the master bedroom.

And the man looked familiar.

His name was Colonel Luc Pierre Essam.

As soon as Bolan saw him, he brought the shotgun around and pumped two more loads of buckshot into the broad-shouldered man's chest. He collapsed to the floor, dead, a bloody mess. Crossing the hall to the smaller bedroom, Bolan checked the bed and closet. Both empty, as was the bathroom between the two bedrooms. And the master bedroom, with two closets and a king-size bed, appeared vacant, too. But when he looked up at the acoustical ceiling, the Executioner saw that one of the panels was slightly ajar.

As he strode toward the panel, Bolan's mind returned to the coffee warehouse. When he was directly beneath the plastic square, he dropped the shotgun, drew his Desert Eagle, then reached up with his free hand and yanked the panel down and out of the ceiling.

Former Cameroonian President Robert Menye started to

fall from the ceiling, then caught himself. But in doing so, he had to let go of the Browning Hi-Power in his hand.

Grabbing the man's throat, Bolan jerked him down to the carpet. The former president landed on his hands and knees and, with his head down, began to cry like a baby.

"Please do not kill me," he pleaded.

The Executioner grabbed the back of the man's head and jerked his face up to meet his own. Tears were rolling down the cowardly ex-president's cheeks as he continued to beg for his life.

Bolan almost couldn't resist the anger that spread through him. He stared down at the man, pressing the barrel of the big .44 against his head. Sobs and pleas for mercy kept coming from the man, and Bolan tightened his grip on the pistol. He thought of the thousands of murders for which this monster was responsible, and every fiber in his body screamed at him to pull the trigger and end the man's life right there and then.

But he didn't.

Robert Menye was not the only dictator practicing genocide in this world, and perhaps a trial like the one Saddam Hussein had undergone would get that fact across to the people of all countries.

So the Executioner let up on the trigger. But he made himself a promise. If worse came to worst, and Menye was freed through some technicality in his trial, the Executioner would track him down and kill him.

Bolan didn't have any handcuffs.

But the Desert Eagle striking the side of Menye's head made the man even more compliant than the restraints would have.

Epilogue

Robert Menye was on his way to the International Criminal Court under heavy guard, and the KDNP and CPU candidates were waiting out their final days at the cottages, surrounded not only by the U.S. Secret Service, but also by roughly one hundred more Cameroonian soldiers handpicked by Jean Antangana and his brother Paul. Neither of the Cameroonian political parties/terrorist organizations had thought to revisit where they'd already been. And even if they did, they would be far outmanned and outgunned.

Bolan and Lareby had entered the airplane provided by Stony Man, and Grimaldi was preparing for takeoff when the Executioner's sat phone rang.

"Cooper," Bolan said as he pushed the button.

"I truly believe it *is* a miracle from God," Jean Antangana said into the phone as Bolan settled into one of the reclining chairs on the airplane. "My cancer is in remission. The doctors cannot explain it."

"Congratulations," the Executioner said into his cell phone as the big plane gathered speed in preparation for takeoff. "I'm happy for you." He buckled his seat belt and leaned back slightly. "And I'm happy for Cameroon. The presidential election is in two days. You *are* planning to file, aren't you?"

"I am," the prime minister said. "And I think that even if I was not in remission, I would file anyway. I have learned a lot over the past several days. One of them is that Cameroon deserves a good and fair president—even if it is only for a short time."

"That's right," Bolan said. "Worry about today today, and tomorrow tomorrow. I only wish I was eligible to vote for you."

Antangana laughed. "I will see that you are granted Cameroonian citizenship any time you desire it, my dear friend."

"Thanks," Bolan said. "But I'm afraid I'm red, white and blue through and through."

As the jet rose in the air and leveled off, Bolan ended the call and looked across the circle of chairs to where Lareby had already fallen asleep. The man was a good agent, but he wasn't used to the kind of hours the Executioner kept.

Bolan unbuckled his seat belt, stood up and walked to the refrigerator bolted to the side of the plane. Taking out a bottle of water, he walked up to the cabin and sat in the copilot's seat next to Grimaldi, who was behind the controls. "How long until we get home, Jack?"

Grimaldi glanced at him, then back at the sky. "Why don't you go back and get some sleep?" he said. "You look like a weekend drunk coming down on Monday morning."

The soldier laughed. "Thanks, Jack," he said. "You've always been a great one for compliments. And I'll take your advice and go to sleep in a few minutes. But how long do you figure we have back to the U.S.?"

"Go on, big guy," Grimaldi said. "Get some rest. You deserve it."

Bolan stared at the pilot. "Okay, Jack," he said. "What is it you aren't telling me?"

Grimaldi exhaled noisily. "I was hoping you'd get some sleep before I had to tell you this."

"I'm a big boy, Jack," Bolan said. "Lay it on me."

"We aren't going home," the Stony Man pilot said. "There's a job in Panama that needs doing first. It's a simple deal, and won't take much briefing. But it's got to be done."

Bolan chuckled. "Then you're right."

"What do you mean?" Grimaldi asked.

"I'd better get some rest."

"I told Hal I'd wake you thirty minutes before we land. He said that would be plenty of time for him to brief you over the phone. And he knows you'll agree to take on this one."

"Fair enough," Bolan said as he returned to the rear of the jet.

Lareby had started to snore as the Executioner closed his eyes. He had fought evil most of his adult life. There was still plenty of it out there, and the future looked as if the war against terrorists, mobsters, Third World despots and other criminals wasn't going to end soon. But he'd be there every time the call to duty came. Count on it.

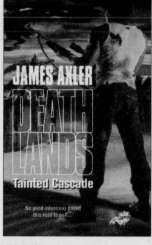